Faking It

Faking It

A NOVEL

ELISA LORELLO

MARINER BOOKS
HOUGHTON MIFFLIN HARCOURT
BOSTON   NEW YORK

First Mariner Books edition 2011

Text copyright © 2010 Elisa Lorello

For information about permission to reproduce selections from this
book, write to Permissions, Houghton Mifflin Harcourt Publishing
Company, 215 Park Avenue South, New York, New York 10003.

www.hmhbooks.com

First published in 2010 by AmazonEncore

Library of Congress Cataloging-in-Publication Data is available.

ISBN 978-0-547-74497-1

Printed in the United States of America

DOC 10 9 8 7 6 5 4 3 2 1

ALSO BY ELISA LORELLO

Ordinary World (a sequel to *Faking It*)

Why I Love Singlehood

For Ru

Prostitution is the oldest profession in the world.
Rhetoric is the second oldest.

——— ———

Faking It

ONE

February

I GATHERED MY BOOKS, pens, student essays, water bottle, coat, and purse as the students sauntered out five minutes early, leaving behind muddy sneaker prints and lackluster enthusiasm. It happens to the best of us at one time or another: we have a bad class, we bomb, we put our students to sleep. Today one of them actually snored.

With a briefcase and a tote bag slung over one shoulder apiece, I exited the musty room as the next class of students—poli-sci, I think—began filing in. My day was done; at least the teaching part was. Three stacks of essays awaited my zealous reading and feedback. "Zealous" was an overstatement; at best, I could get about five essays done per hour, three hours max. And I needed breaks in between. If only our brains had scanning machines. If only mind melds really worked. It's my dirty little secret that I'd rather be looking at *The Simpsons* than Shakespeare. I know I'm inches from being found out, about everything...

I'd moved back to Long Island because Maggie, my best friend and former colleague from South Coast Community College in Massachusetts, was now director of the writing program at Brooklyn University and offered me a position assisting her and teaching full-time. Maggie and I had collaborated on a number of projects and articles at SCCC (my favorite being the one we never submitted for publication but wrote to blow off steam: "Fuck the Modes: We Want Artifacts!"). We'd spend hours in her office, discussing composition theory and pedagogy and Wendy Bishop articles and what it was really like to work with Lad Tobin ("the Woody Allen of rhetoric and composition," I call him). She always knew when I was approaching her office by the rhythm and sound my shoes made on the carpet. We were allies, colleagues, and friends all at the same time. I couldn't resist the chance to work with her again.

So, that was the reason. (Oh yeah, and I also broke up with my fiancé...)

———

I'd been back on the Island for only six months, and frankly, I was surprised at how long it was taking me to adjust. I'd been away for ten years, living in a small town in southeastern Massachusetts (small by Long Island's standards, at least). Fairhaven echoed faint similarities to the Northport of my youth and young adulthood: split-level housing developments on cul-de-sacs, nearby shopping centers and malls minutes from the parkway (although in Massachusetts they call it the "highway"), and a reasonable driving distance to and from both the city and the ocean. The familiarity felt comfortable.

I used to think the Island was life affirming. Perhaps because it was home. Or maybe it was the "Mini-Me" of Manhattan. Whatever it was, I had spent the last ten years writing about and romancing Long Island from my Massachusetts digs. I wrote about the roads, the beaches, the shopping, the people, the accents, the sports teams, the Hamptons, you name it. But now that I was back and paying a thousand dollars more in rent for a thousand less square feet of space, I couldn't for the life of me figure out what was so energizing about this strap-on to the Big Apple and its wannabe inhabitants. Nevertheless, I took the job at Brooklyn U and a residential apartment in East Meadow, about fifteen minutes away from the Long Island Railroad, and the cost of commuting was killing me each month. Some days I would drive all the way to Brooklyn; other days I'd drive to the train station, take the train to Queens, and switch to the subway. I'd forgotten how everything on Long Island was high-maintenance. When you put a high-maintenance woman in a low-maintenance town, the woman just stands out as having it all together. Put that same woman back into the town that made her high-maintenance to begin with, and you've simply got another stressed-out New Yorker, no different from anyone else. Now I found myself missing—and writing about—the small shores of West Island Beach, the slow service of Pop's Coffeehouse, and the shrill sounds of New England accents.

But that was all I had, it seemed. Memories.

It's not that I didn't look for anything else. I kept an eye out for single professors when I attended seminars or campus workshops on writing across the curriculum, or evenings spent at poetry readings in coffee shops. No matter where I went, though, unavailability was everywhere.

Men were married, involved, divorced with children, too old, too young, or gay. They were Republican, unemployed, or mama's boys. They were atheists and Giants fans. And I couldn't help but wonder if I was projecting an unavailability of my own. Because none of them were Andrew.

———

Nothing to watch tonight, nowhere to go, nothing in the fridge, nothing in my wallet. Essays to read, laundry to do, bills to pay, rooms to clean, and the dust was forming its own kind of woven fabric on the furniture. No calls, e-mails, letters.

My God, there has to be something better than this. This is not enough. Not anymore.

I thought that as I walked through the hallways, down the icy sidewalks, and to the train.

And that's when it all began.

TWO

March

WESTFORD-LANGLEY PUBLISHING company was hosting a seminar and textbook fair in the city. This one focused on the latest applications of electronic portfolios in the composition classroom. Maggie and I loved these kinds of seminars—they gave us a chance to talk about theory, meet and reunite with some of our favorite people in academia, check out the new textbooks on the market, and socialize. She and Jayce, our colleague and friend, sat in my office on the matching high-back chairs that I'd picked up at a Salvation Army rummage sale for twenty dollars apiece. Maggie was tall—almost five foot ten—and broad shouldered with a long torso and long legs. She wore her hair straight and bottle-blond, with wire-framed glasses and flawless MAC makeup. Her appearance was intimidating and her voice was deep and full, yet her personality was kitten-like. Jayce, on the other hand, was paper-thin petite with smooth, dark skin, and very, very chic. A lifelong Brooklynite, one would take her for a fashion magazine editor rather than a writing professor.

"Andi, come with us to the cocktail party after the seminar," Jayce said.

"I don't know; cocktail parties aren't my thing," I replied.

"She doesn't drink," Maggie explained.

"So what?"

"So, I don't want to be the only sober one. Come on, you know those things. They're meat markets and show-off fests, and the more intoxicated you are the more likely you'll get hit on by Joe Doolittle and not mind it."

"Might be worth it if he has tenure," Jayce said.

"I won't drink either," Maggie offered. Mags was the type of person who would give you a hundred dollars if you casually mentioned you needed to buy a hundred lottery tickets to increase your chances of winning.

"Just come," Jayce said again. "You don't have to drink. People-watch. It's a great time to network."

You can always convince me to network.

The cocktail party followed the seminar two hours later at the National Arts Club in Gramercy Park. Most of the seminar attendees stuck around, making a weekend of it. Maggie, Jayce, and I found a small Thai place for a quick dinner before returning to the club to freshen up. We entered fashionably late, of course. Jayce immediately began to mingle, a cosmopolitan already in her hand. Maggie ordered a wine spritzer. I slowly sipped a ginger ale. We found a high-legged table that was not too centered in the room yet not too removed from the crowd. We sat for a while, invited people to join us and talk teaching for a bit, then people-watched.

"You know, John Kirkland is not as tall as he looks when he's at the podium," I remarked, watching him yukking it up with two professors from NYU.

"You're right. And did you notice the snorting noise he makes when he's about to begin a new thought?"

I tried to stifle my laugh, but it came just as I sipped my drink, and thus I began both a laughing and coughing fit while the carbonation pinched my nostrils. Just then, as I smeared ginger ale from the front of my shirt, I saw him enter the room with one of the textbook reps: Tall. Six feet, maybe a few inches to spare. Mid to late thirties, possibly. He wore a taupe-colored suit—Versace, I think—with a finely woven shirt underneath. Alluring, to say the least. His dark hair fell forward in wispy layers yet stayed close to the nape of his neck. Perfect for running my fingers through, I thought. Olive skinned, yet could also be booth tanned—hard to tell in the lighting. When another rep greeted the couple, he flashed a smile that sent sparks from his—what were they, brown eyes? Regardless of color, they had transfixed me in the split second of that smile.

"Who is that guy with Allison?" I asked. "I didn't see him at the seminar."

"I don't know," Maggie replied, "but he's gorgeous, isn't he. Maybe he's her husband?"

"Let's mingle," I said, and got up to walk around. I chimed in on conversations about Trimbur's newest article and the memorial for the late Donald Murray and what's going on at Brooklyn U and had I heard any good gossip about SCCC lately. All the while I tracked Versace with my peripheral vision, like a hidden camera. I watched him schmooze with professors, sip his drink, and turn every woman's head in the room. What's more, I watched some of the women exchange knowing glances with each other, almost like a secret handshake, behind his back.

I had to find out who he was.

I approached another rep.

"Great job today, Carol."

"Thanks, Andi."

Carol stood about five foot five and had audacious, red-orange hair that fell past her shoulders. She was pale and thin, in her forties, and wore silk scarves with every combination of business pinstripe pant or skirt suit.

I leaned in to her, underneath the chatter. "So who's the guy with Allison?" Her saleswoman smile turned into a sly grin, like the cat that not only ate the canary but also had a smoke afterwards. "Is he her husband?" I asked.

She guffawed, "Good gracious, no!"

"Then who is he?"

"Let me put it to you this way: he's her 'cocktail party companion.'"

"So then, he's not with a university?"

Now she was laughing at my expense, and I felt my face get hot.

"No. But he's probably been with almost every female professor in this room."

I choked on my ginger ale for the second time.

"Excuse me?" I sputtered.

"He's Allison's cocktail party date, but he's also Wanda's New Year's Eve date, Joanne's every-third-Saturday-of-the-month date, and Sadie's I-need-a-good-lay date." I still looked at her blankly, and she finally cut to the chase: "He's an escort."

While Carol moved on to the next conversation, I searched for and found Maggie with a small group of postmodernists from Long Island College and pulled her aside when a lull in the chat appeared.

I leaned in and whispered, "He's an *escort*, Mags! Can you *believe* that?"

"You're kidding!"

"Nope, Carol just told me. Do you think maybe she's putting me on?"

"I don't know. How do we find out?"

"Well, according to Carol, apparently he gets around the lecture circuit more than we do."

"He's been watching you, you know," Maggie said.

I looked at her, agog. "Are you kidding me?"

"I saw him take notice of you before, and then a few minutes ago when you crossed the room to talk to me. He actually looked up from whoever—*whom*ever—no, *who*ever—"

"*What*ever..."

"—he was talking to."

"Why?"

"What do you mean, why?"

I didn't answer her. Instead, I went to the bar to get another ginger ale, where I heard a sonorous, baritone voice behind me.

"Enjoying the party?"

I whipped around, and there was Versace, flashing another smile. I practically had to crane my neck to look him in the eye, he was so tall. God, his eyes were incredible. Not brown. Sienna.

"Yeah, it's been a long time since I've been to one of these," I said.

"Are you driving tonight?"

I looked at him, perplexed. "I'm sorry?"

"You've been nursing that ginger ale all night. I was wondering if you were a designated driver."

"No, I took the train in from the Island, but I'm staying with a colleague in Brooklyn tonight."

Why did I call her a colleague and not a friend? Did I want to sound more like a professional and less like a schoolgirl at a dance?

"I'm Devin," he said, extending his hand.

What the hell kind of name is Devin?

"Andrea," I replied. His shake was sturdy, without squeezing. I quickly scanned his hand: he manicured his nails.

"What university do you teach at?"

"I just came to Brooklyn U about six months ago."

"And you live on the Island?"

"Yeah, just moved back after ten years in New England."

"Wow," he said. "I'd like to see the foliage up there in the fall."

"Yeah," I replied, indulging his small talk, "it's really beautiful."

Geez, how long does it take to get a ginger ale?

"So," I said, "I saw you with Allison? She's the rep who invited us here. My colleague and I are putting together a deal to write a textbook for her company—"

"Just a friend," he interrupted. As the words came out of his mouth, Allison approached, a younger carbon copy of Carol minus the silk scarves, looking at the both of us with daggers. Just a friend, my ass…

"Well, I didn't ask. But now that you mention it, I think your friend wants your attention."

He looked at her and signaled that he was getting her a drink. Then he winked at her. What a player, I thought. Gorgeous, yes. But way too into himself.

Allison then practically stood between us. "Honey, I'd like to get going soon, OK?"

"Sure, Ali," he said before he kissed her on the cheek and put his arm around her. I couldn't be sure from the angle I was standing, but I thought I saw her give his rear left cheek a squeeze, like Charmin.

"It was nice to meet you, Andrea. Welcome back to New York." He shook my hand again.

In the six months since I'd been home, no one—not even my mother—had welcomed me back.

"You too," I replied as he and Allison walked away arm in arm. I saw Maggie grinning at me.

"What did he say to you?" she asked when I walked back to her.

"He's a jerk," I replied. "He just wanted to pick me up."

"How do you know?"

I didn't know. I'd just assumed.

"He insisted that he and Allison were 'just friends.' Give me a break. He's a charmer."

"Well, he must be good at it."

"Yeah, well, everyone needs a skill."

"I did some research, and apparently he does really get around. And you're right—he *is* an escort. 'Bout a year ago, one of the reps bragged about him to a professor, and the next thing you know, he's the hot commodity. Even Jayce knew of him. She never, you know, *used* him, or anything like that. But she's seen him with the others. I just wanna know how *we* stayed out of the loop for so long," she said, pointing between the two of us.

"What does he do? I mean, does he just go on dates? Or does he do more?"

"Judging by the look of these women's faces, I'd say he does *everything*."

For sure, this guy would never get past my front door.

Maggie lived in a one-bedroom apartment in Brooklyn, about six blocks away from the university, and I often crashed at her place whenever we attended an event in the city. Later that evening, as I snuggled under the faded, folk-style quilt on her couch, I thought about Devin and his smile. Those sparks that flickered in the specks of his pupils. That Versace suit and finely woven mock-neck. I thought about our brief conversation, replayed it in my mind. Wondered what I could've or should've said to him. Coulda-woulda-shoulda. Moments later, as I drifted off to sleep, Devin visited me in a dream. And he disappeared almost as quickly as he had earlier at the bar.

THREE

April

S PRING BREAK CAME and went, and I did nothing
more exciting than a day trip to East Hampton for
window-shopping with Maggie (we couldn't really afford to do much else), while Jayce went on a Bahaman
cruise. I'd pretty much stayed away from the city and
shacked up in my apartment, cleaning and de-cluttering
it. I could cover the walls of an East End mansion just
out of the paper I'd accumulated that seemingly repro-
duced like bunnies. At one point, while on my knees
scrubbing a stain out of the living room carpet, I felt the
urge to sing, *Some day my prince will come* . . . God, how
pathetic.

Spring weather came early this year, and I started
taking my classes outside to the courtyard, a landscaped
blanket of grass and benches and little trees with a fountain at its nucleus, all encircled by concrete walkways
leading to every building that took up about a five-block
radius of the city. (Brooklyn, I mean. We New Yorkers call
every inch of land covered in the five boroughs "the city";
we call Long Island "New York"; and everything else is
"Upstate.") Surprisingly, the students remained attentive
and even productive. Some wrote furiously, freewriting

about places they'd like to visit, places they'd never seen, and places they never wanted to see again. And I joined them, getting lost in my own prose, remembering long walks on Rocky Beach with Andrew. I was missing him lately, re-tracing his hazel eyes that slit in sunlight; his blondish brown, wavy hair that fell past his shoulders; and his soft hands. For a guitar player, he had exceptionally soft hands. You'd think they'd be rugged and calloused, but no. In fact, he had the softest hands of any man I'd ever known. How I loved holding those hands. How I loved when those hands strummed his twelve-string guitar and serenaded me with James Taylor and Cat Stevens and Paul Simon, even though I didn't particularly care for James Taylor or Cat Stevens or Paul Simon. How I loved when those hands glided down my cheek and across my bare back and along my thigh…

"Professor Cutrone?"

I looked up. Steven, a student from Maine and still wearing a wool cap from winter that fell past his ears, interrupted my fantasy, as well as my freewrite.

"Yes?"

He lowered his raised hand. "Are we going to read these aloud?"

I paused and looked down at the ode to Andrew I was scribbling and felt a quick hot flash.

"Nope."

———

Allison, the Westford-Langley rep, had just come out of Maggie's office, juggling textbooks, when I nearly bumped into her in the hallway, both of us gasping a "Whoops!" followed by apologies.

"Walk with me, Andi. I've got a new edition to show you." She held out the updated edition of a writing-across-the-curriculum book and explained its added features while I flipped through the text and half listened to her, imagining her with Devin, wondering what they did together after the cocktail party and how far they had gotten. When an image of the two of them naked in a shower stall permeated the picture, I spoke up and handed the book back to her.

"So tell me about that guy Devin you were with at the seminar a couple of months ago. I was just wondering if the rumors are true."

She shot me a glance, and I was afraid that I'd struck a nerve, forgetting how jealous she'd looked when she saw us talking at the bar in the National Arts Club that night.

"What have you heard?" she asked.

"I heard he's an escort."

"Yes, and a damn good one, too. You want his number?"

I turned sharply to look at her. "You don't mind?"

"Of course not. He's not my fiancé or anything like that."

"You seemed a little miffed when you saw us talking that night."

"I did? Well, that's just because I pay him plenty to talk to *me*. I can't help but get possessive when he's mine for the night."

"Where'd you meet him?" I asked.

"Delia gave me his card."

"Delia Howard? The dean?"

"Yeah, that was nice of her, wasn't it? She met him through the rep from Ashton Press and then went out with him the following week to a Broadway premiere, and the rest is history."

"Are all his clients in academia?"

"Well, word's gotten around to a lot of us. But he's got 'em all over the city in all kinds of jobs, mostly high-end. You know, corporate women, lawyers… We have a great time together, and he's a-*ma*-zing, if you know what I mean." She said the second part in a hushed voice. I didn't know how to respond to that, so I simply said, "I'll bet."

I braced myself for my next question: "Um, what does he do?"

"You want a list?" she laughed.

"How much does he charge?"

She leaned in close and whispered the amount in my ear. My mouth dropped open.

"Did I hear you right?"

"If you have to ask, you did." I looked at Allison in disbelief—not because of the amount she had just quoted but because I had no idea textbook reps made that much money. The dean, yes. And what about my colleagues? Were they partners in some stock deal?

"How often do you use him—I mean, see him?" I asked

"Not enough. Face it: he is pricey. He's also really busy, getting busier all the time. Sometimes he works straight through the week. I had to make my date with him for the seminar a month in advance."

"Not even off on Sundays for a day of rest?"

"Andi, this guy is *good*."

"He seemed kinda arrogant when I met him."

"He is definitely a charmer. But give him a chance. He's actually quite intelligent and holds a good conversation. Here…" She stopped in her tracks, reached into her over-the-shoulder briefcase, pulled out a pouch bursting with business cards, sifted through the deck, and found the one she was looking for. She handed it to me. STRAWBERRIES AND CHAMPAGNE blazed in fire-engine-red letters, with a phone number in Century Gothic type underneath. "It's a message service. Leave your name and number and someone will call you back—usually Devin's partner. There are five guys total. Be sure to specify that you want Devin."

"He owns the business?"

"Yeah. Self-starter."

I stared at the card some more. She said, "Trust me. It's like finding a good therapist."

"Or a good mechanic," I added.

"You'll never want to go back to conventional dating, for one thing. Who needs the aggravation? He's safe, he's respectful, and he's sexy. What more could you want? And you don't have to nag him to take out the garbage or mow the lawn or any of that crap."

I never had to do that; then again, with the exception of Andrew, I was never with a man long enough to get to that stage. Besides, Andrew lived in a condo, and we broke up just as we decided to move in together and started house hunting… *What am I thinking?*

"Don't you need this?" I asked, holding the card out to her.

She shook her head. "Keep it. I've got him on speed-dial on my cell."

Later that evening, in my apartment, I tacked Devin's card on my bulletin board above my computer and stared at it. *There is no way you are going to call this guy. You can't afford him. And besides, you don't* do *stuff like that.* I then resumed my rapid typing, but the hot red letters burned right through the screen. I did my best to avert my eyes and focus on the monitor; but I didn't get much work done.

———

Dating in New York is more like an anthropological study of mating rituals of a certain cultural species. There's no excuse for sitting home any night of the week other than being in traction. I'd been to more cocktail parties in the first three months since I'd returned than in the ten years I lived in Massachusetts. Granted, I was no longer a poor graduate student, or worse, an adjunct treated like a second-class citizen, so I could afford nights out. But still. Despite the fact that I had lived thirty minutes from Providence and an hour from Boston, a night out in New England consisted of a movie at the Fairhaven Bijou with Andrew or dinner at the Bayside restaurant in Westport, followed by walks on the beach. Come winter, everyone holed up in their propane-heated nests and hosted their own dinner parties so they wouldn't have to go out in the cold to someone else's.

New York City, however, was the quintessential cornucopia of places to go and people to meet, a vortex. Relationships progressed from ten minutes at a bar to a quickie in a cab to a week in the Hamptons to the bridal registry at Bergdorf's, or Macy's if you had to slum it. In Massachusetts, school, friends, and online match sites were the way to meet people. In New York, all you had to do was ride the train, for starters.

But I was never that kind of casual dater; I never trusted anyone. I avoided eye contact with everyone on the train, and whenever someone wanted to set me up with a friend or colleague, I insisted on enforcing the Patriot Act and getting hold of his library reading list, Netflix orders, dental records, prior convictions, you name it. Most of my exes had started as friends I'd either met through coworkers or classmates. Andrew was part of the SCCC faculty, an adjunct like me, and we'd met at an orientation meeting a week before my second semester began. I'd watched him from the other side of the classroom, sitting quietly but listening intently to one of the tenure-track professors drone on about academic integrity of the faculty, and I wondered, *What's his story?* One week later, as I whisked into the English department's main office to check my mail, he was standing at the mailboxes, saw me, and smiled as his eyes brightened.

"Hi! You were at the meeting, weren't you?"

"Yeah, I was."

"I really liked your ideas about peer review."

"Thanks," I said, half listening, finding an empty mailbox and turning to leave. I was halfway down the hall when a voice in my head said, *Pay attention!* He followed me out.

"I'm Andrew."

"Andi."

"I prefer Andrew."

"No, I mean, my name is Andrea; people call me Andi."

"Oh," he said, furrowing his brows (probably thinking, *This is going to make for some dumb jokes down the road*). "Maybe we can get together for coffee sometime and brainstorm ideas for assignments?"

I looked at him. He was lanky and wore jeans with dress shirts and ties. Normally, I thought most guys looked dorky in such attire, but on him it looked cute.

"Sure," I said. My stomach had fluttered the moment I'd said it, and I smiled back at him.

When I found out that he played the guitar, I knew I was doomed.

And that's how our fourteen-month relationship began. I moved back to New York less than six months after we broke up; just passing him in the hallway was too much for me to bear.

Since then, I'd gone out with Maggie and Jayce and met lots of guys; yet, most of those times my friends had to coax me out with promises of dessert or payment of my subway fare (which they almost never did). But dating was a whole other story. Dating was a jungle too scary for me to safari through. Being a stay-at-home, single woman had devolved from a New England comfort to a New York refuge.

———

One month later, the semester ended in its usual hustle of weeklong student conferences followed by weeklong portfolio reading and grading sessions followed by weeklong meetings on program assessment and reflection and projections. Along with the end of the semester came the end-of-semester party that was usually held at the Heartland Brewery in Union Square. Apparently a couple of professors who lived nearby had started the tradition of meeting there so that they wouldn't have far to go after they'd gotten plastered. Once again, Maggie and I took the train in together and joined our colleagues. Immediately I spotted Devin at the bar, this time wearing black (Versace again), and my insides tightened as I stiffened my lower back. I hadn't seen him since the seminar. I was dressed in my favorite blue jeans, a black T-shirt with a fraying, thrift store–bought, men's velvet blazer, and black leather boots. My hair was straight and shiny and fell in wispy flips. I glanced in his direction, trying to be as subtle as possible, nudging Maggie on the arm.

"Look who's here," I said under my breath.

"Ooh, is that the male hooker?" Maggie asked. "Wonder who he's with." Before I had a chance to investigate, he caught my eye, smiled, and started to walk toward me. As Maggie nudged me back, my abdominal muscles pulled even tighter as I began to tremble. Even the hellos from my female colleagues and their attempts to block his path to steal a free moment with him didn't slow him down. The male professors looked at him resentfully, and no wonder. He was perfection. Michelangelo would've dropped his chisel and cut off his hands if he saw Devin.

"Hi!" he said jubilantly. "Remember me? We met at a cocktail party a few months ago." He sounded a lot like Andrew did that day in the department main office.

"Yeah, I remember you. It was back in February at the National Arts Club. I can't remember your name, though," I lied.

"Devin." He extended his hand for a new handshake. "You are..." He paused for a minute and closed his eyes as his memory performed a quick search. "Andrea?"

My eyes widened. "Wow, I'm surprised you remembered!"

"I have a good memory for names. It's good for business. So, Andrea..."

"Most people call me Andi."

"What brings you here this evening?"

"End-of-semester party. And you?"

"I was meeting a client for drinks, but I think I've been stood up. Can I get you a ginger ale while you're waiting for the rest of your party to come in?"

Geez, he even remembered the ginger ale. I turned to Maggie with a get-me-out-of-this expression and grew self-conscious as my colleagues watched me talking to Devin, eyebrows raised, certain they were thinking I'd hired him for the night, or previous nights.

"Listen," I said, moving away from the crowd and pulling him with me. "I know what you do for a living. And if you're trying to recruit me as a client, well, I'm not interested. First of all, I couldn't afford you. And second of all, I don't do—I'm not that kind of... I'm not interested, OK?"

You know that voice in your head, the one that screams at you like your third-grade soccer coach as you've just kicked the ball into your own goal by mistake: *What kind of shmuck are you?* Devin confirmed my shmuckness with his twisted grin. He stood there and let me ramble. When I finally stopped, he spoke.

"For the record, I don't recruit—I have more than enough business. You look like an interesting person to talk to, that's all."

"Isn't that a conflict of interest?"

He started laughing as I felt my face turn a shade of burgundy that matched the glass of wine in his hand.

"That's cute," he said. "I'm sorry; I don't mean to embarrass you. Are you uncomfortable with me?"

"Well, yeah."

"Look, Andi. I just wanted to say hello. Sorry if I made you uncomfortable. I'll let you get back to your colleagues."

He waved to them. They all waved back, with flirty, white-toothed smiles and their chests sticking out.

I stood there, my feet cemented to the floor.

"OK."

Neither of us moved.

"It was nice to see you again. I like your hair like that, by the way," he said.

"You too."

Dear Lord, kill me now. Please.

"See ya."

Devin finally walked away, and I unstuck my feet and headed for the ladies' room, shaking as I looked into the mirror. *Get a grip.* I took several deep breaths and a tissue from my purse; my nose was shiny. When I regained my composure, I took one last look in the mirror and looked at my hair: not a strand of my neo-shag was out of place.

Chestnut brown and landing slightly past the bottom of my neck, it looked as if I'd just come out of the stylist's chair. He liked it like this. A smile escaped me as I exited the ladies' room.

FOUR

June

FOR THE LAST five years in Massachusetts, I had taught
summer school English at a public high school. A
year after Andrew and I started dating, he had signed
up to teach as well. He always stuck to the high school
curriculum; during the last summer we were together, he
had tried to motivate his students to read *The Canterbury
Tales* by converting it into a musical, while I invited my
students to write argumentative essays about why the high
school's mission statement was a crock. Andrew's class
fanned themselves with rolled up Spark Notes booklets,
while my class conducted peer reviews not unlike those I
supervised at the college level. I'd refrained from telling
him that his students were cutting his class to sit in on
mine.

"I don't get it, Cutch," he said one afternoon in Pop's
Coffeehouse, sweaty and deflated. "I'm not getting anywhere with them. I thought taking a fresh approach would
help."

"It's *summer*, hon," I said, sipping my iced vanilla chai.
"Without air-conditioning in the classrooms, you couldn't
even get them excited about *American Idol*."

By the time I detoxed from the academic year, then prepped for summer school, then detoxed from that, then prepped for the upcoming semester, I hardly had time to sit down and write anything. But here in New York, I looked forward to my first full summer vacation stretched out ahead of me just like my students did. Except rather than go to the beach and work on future melanomas, I had excitedly planned to catch up on writing a collection of creative nonfiction essays and reading journal articles, not to mention Maggie's and my textbook project.

At the moment, however, I sat in front of my computer in my apartment surfing the Internet, with a floor-stand fan whirring loudly and rotating from left to right and left again. I was bored, tired, and lonely, and hadn't written a damn thing—heck, I might as well have been sitting in Andrew's summer English class, sweating and listening to him ramble on about *A Midsummer Night's Dream* and extol the virtues of the mandolin, trying not to pass out from dehydration.

I started looking through personal ads and match sites:

- Smart is sexy! Intelligent WF seeks educated WM for long conversations into the night.
- Trim SJM seeks slim SJF for good times.
- Books, beaches, and basketball are what this woman likes. No unemployed men, please.
- I love women with curves! Come meet this lonely, 40-year-old male. No kids or smoking.

Oy.

I looked up at the bulletin board cluttered with Post-it notes for essay and memoir ideas; phone numbers and e-mail addresses of friends and textbook editors; photos of my two brothers, Joey and Tony; Maggie and me at the Language Arts Conference in Chicago two years ago; and one of Andrew and me, with Andrew's face scratched out. (I had kept it up as a reminder whenever I started to miss him.) Devin's card was still tacked up.

My phone sat in its cradle next to the computer. My eyes shifted back and forth from the phone to the card. Finally, I picked it up and dialed. After two rings, a voice mail answered, just as I was told. When it beeped, I began:

"Hi, uh, this message is for Devin? Uh, this is Doctor Andi Cutrone. From Brooklyn University? We, uh, met a few times? I was wondering if I could, uh, talk to you? Uh, please call me at this number…"

Oh, that was smooth…and why the hell did I use "doctor"? Three years to get a PhD, and this was what I reserved my title for—leaving messages for escorts on hot June days?

Two hours later, Devin returned the call.

"A colleague gave me your number," I said with a wavering voice. "I hope that's OK."

"Sure, it's fine. What can I do for you?"

"Well, I'd like to meet with you, but not as a business meeting."

"What do you mean?"

"I mean I just want a consultation."

After what seemed like a long pause, he laughed.

"That's cute," he said. "OK." I could hear his smile over the phone. "Why don't we meet at the W Hotel?"

"I live on the Island, remember? Is there something a little more in the middle? How 'bout Junior's in Brooklyn?" I wasn't too keen on taking the drive, but it was fair. Besides, it'd been a while since I'd had a slice of cheesecake.

"OK. When?"

"What's good for you?" I asked.

"Weekdays between one and four work for me."

"Let's make it two o'clock on Tuesday."

"I'm entering you in my BlackBerry," he said.

"Me too," I said, scribbling on a napkin.

"Thanks. See you then."

I hung up the phone. My heart was racing.

What the hell are you smiling at?

———

I'd spent the days leading up to Tuesday trying to keep myself distracted—shopping at the Roosevelt Field Mall, trying on outfit after outfit (nothing, and I mean *nothing* looked good on me—I did not have a body for summer clothes), going to Jones Beach and drenching myself in sunblock for fear of getting a blistery sunburn and showing up at Junior's with a face akin to bubble wrap, and even going out to lunch with my mother one day, which goes to show how anxious I really was, although I said nothing to her about it—even Maggie didn't know about this meeting.

The smell of baked goods and coffee wafted through my nostrils as I flung open the door to Junior's. Located two blocks down and around the corner from the Brooklyn U campus, Junior's Restaurant was a New York icon, as familiar to Brooklynites as the Brooklyn Bridge, or Ebbets Field once upon a time. Its autumn colored décor offset by black-and-white photos of the city was inviting enough, but the cheesecake—oh, the cheesecake! When restaurants in Massachusetts touted their "New York cheesecake," I knew they were hoping, praying that it might be worthy enough to be as tasty as a Junior's cheesecake left on someone's fork (and how there could be any trace of leftover Junior's cheesecake on someone's fork was beyond my comprehension). They served regular food, too, although I couldn't for the life of me remember anything on the menu. When I had first stumbled across Junior's Web site from which one could order a cheesecake to be shipped to just about anywhere in the country, I almost resented it, like a kid reluctant to let her friends play with her Barbie Townhouse and Corvette. Some things were meant to be coveted, savored, and shared with as few people as possible. (Just so long as I was one of the included, I guessed.) Some things shouldn't be so available—you had to work for it. That way, you could appreciate it even more.

Even in the middle of the day, the place bustled with busboys, waitstaff, and patrons of all nations. As I waited to be seated and took a swig of water from the plastic bottle I always carried with me, I felt a light tap on my shoulder. I whisked around and instantly contracted the muscles of my mouth to refrain from a full-blown smile, but it was too late. The water dribbled from the side of my mouth and onto my shirt.

"Hey," I said, knowing I had already blown playing it cool. I capped and shoved the bottle into my Westford-Langley tote bag.

"Hi." He wore vintage Gap jeans and a faded midnight blue T-shirt, and his hair was tousled with pomade (and clearly Versace wasn't the only thing he looked good in). I, on the other hand, felt frumpy in light cream capris and a brown scoop-neck T-shirt, and was having a bad hair day thanks to the morning humidity.

We were seated at a booth, and without looking at a menu, I ordered a slice of plain cheesecake, my mouth already salivating for it, while he ordered coffee and rugelach. At first we made small talk.

"So, how long have you been back to New York?" he asked me.

"It'll be a year on August first," I answered. "I grew up in Northport, though."

"No kidding! I should've known you were a North Shore girl. I'm from Massapequa."

"I should've known you were a South Shore guy."

"I'll bet we went to the same dance clubs in Hempstead back in the early nineties."

God, I hoped not.

"What made you move back here?" he asked. "Certainly it wasn't a better cost of living."

"No, but it was a better job offer. I got my PhD and needed full-time, and my good friend Maggie—"

"The one you were hanging out with at the National Arts Club and the Heartland Brewery..." he interjected.

Freakish memory.

"Yeah, well, she's the director of the first-year writing program at Brooklyn U and needed an assistant, and managed to convince the dean to appoint me without doing a search, being that it was a non-tenure-track position."

"Do you like your job?" he asked.

"A lot."

"Are you good at what you do?"

He asked the question in a way that made me think he already knew the answer, and agreed with me.

"I think so." I paused for a beat and answered more affirmatively, "Yes, I am." On the inside, I smiled; this admission anchored me in a way I hadn't expected.

I mustered up the courage to ask him about his line of work, taking a sip of water from his glass instead of my own by mistake. He was polite enough not to point it out to me, although he looked at the glass and I noticed quickly enough as I felt my face go hot.

"So, how'd you get into the escort business?" I asked, ignoring my blunder.

"Like you, I wanted to do something I was both good at and enjoyed. I enjoy being with women, pleasing women, and I'm good at it. Besides, the money is great."

"What do you do with them?"

"Same thing other couples do. We go to parties, plays— I've seen just about every fucking musical on Broadway— the opera, gallery openings, even a movie once in a while. Then, sometimes I'll give them massages or shampoo their hair..."

"You *shampoo their hair?*" I asked in disbelief.

"Have you ever had your hair shampooed?"

"Of course."

"At eleven o'clock at night in a bubble bath with candles?"

I paused to let my imagination soak in the visual, and felt a sensation not unlike a striking match run up my spine.

"Are you in the bathtub with them?" I asked.

"Not usually. It's more about indulging their pleasure."

"I think they'd be pleased to have you in the tub with them."

Devin shook his head. "Most women just want to be attended to, without worrying about having to give something back. They feel like they're constantly giving so much of themselves, trying to please everyone under the sun." He then leaned in toward me. "What's *your* pleasure, Andi?"

I stiffened and went on the defense. "Are you trying to come on to me?"

He leaned back against the cushioned backrest of the booth seat.

"Man, you are the most uptight person I've ever met, and I barely know you. I've never seen anyone so guarded. Were you raised in a religious household or something?"

"Yes."

"No kidding. What else happened to you?"

I averted my eyes just as the waiter returned with our order.

"Like you said, you barely know me," I said. "And by the way, I think I'm entitled to a little reservation."

I took a bite of cheesecake and chewed very slowly. *Sweet mother of…*

"You're avoiding the question," he said.

"Which question?"

"What's your pleasure?"

"Why do you want to know?"

"It's not something I plan to use against you, if that's what you're worried about. It's a valid question, right up there with what are your dreams in life and where do you see yourself living in five years."

"It may be a valid question, but it's also a personal question. Why should I share my sexual pleasures with you?"

"Who said they had to be sexual? Reading a book can be pleasurable. Riding in a convertible with the top down, every bite of that cheesecake—and I can tell you're enjoying that cheesecake. That cheesecake is absolutely sensual to you, isn't it."

I hate this guy.

"So?" he said. "What're your pleasures?"

I stared at him for a moment, the fork lingering in my mouth.

"OK. You're right about the cheesecake. As far as my other pleasures go, well, I like chocolate; the sound of a really good acoustic guitar; a brisk walk on a warm, breezy day like today; and foot massages. How's that?"

He finished chewing his rugelach. "It's a start. Now, imagine someone feeding you that chocolate, playing your favorite song on that guitar, taking that walk with you—although the walk is a bit cliché, isn't it?—and giving you that foot massage."

Once again I let the image soak in, and once again I felt the striking match. But I kept my guard up.

"I can get that in a serious relationship—why should I have to pay for it?"

"For some women, it's worth paying for. For some women, it's the only way they'll get it. And when was the last time you got it? When was the last time you were in a serious relationship?"

I thought of Andrew and realized that I was the one who gave him the massages, dragged him out for walks, and coaxed him to play me a song.

"So, you're their savior. How nice of you. And all for a price."

"I'm providing a service using my talents—same as you."

"Yeah, but my service is legal."

"My service is completely legal. I'm a companion for the night. The contract states explicitly that I don't—how shall I say this?—go beyond certain boundaries."

"That's not what I heard. I heard you're pretty fucking amazing. And I've seen the looks on these women's faces. Don't tell me that's all from a kiss on the cheek at the end of the night."

"I provide other sorts of pleasure, but you're assuming the rest."

I sat and stared at him for a moment. He both annoyed and intrigued the hell out of me. I didn't know what to say next.

Devin resumed the conversation. "So. Andi. You wanted to consult with me. Now that you've done that, what do you think?"

"I'm not interested."

I was lying. The fact is, I was *really* interested, but how could I tell him what I really wanted? How could I face my colleagues and friends—hell, face myself? And how could I afford it?

"You sure?"

My back stiffened. Did he know?

"Yeah. Sorry to waste your time."

"Not at all. I already knew you weren't going to be a client. But you are a very interesting person to talk to."

Didn't he say that the last time we met?

"What makes you say that?" I asked.

"You're not the type."

"What type is that?" I asked, defensive yet again.

"You care too much about what other people think. You're too self-conscious."

"No—I mean, what makes you say I'm an interesting person to talk to?"

"I don't know—there's something about you, Andi. I noticed you the minute I entered the room, and I just knew I had to talk to you."

He noticed me. By God, he noticed me from the moment he saw me.

My stomach fluttered, and I looked at my watch.

"I should go before traffic gets bad," I said. He looked at me for a moment, as if he were studying me. We stood up, and when we got outside, Devin thanked me and shook my hand yet again, his hand warm. As we parted and walked in opposite directions, something inside tugged at me. *Don't let him leave*, I heard myself say. *What makes you think you've got it so good? For God's sake, do something different!*

I turned and quickly walked, almost breaking into a jog, until I caught up with him and called out his name, somewhat startling him. We stopped in the middle of the sidewalk in front of a Laundromat.

"Suppose I wanted you to teach me a few things."

His eyes widened as he smiled slyly. "Like what?"

My insides churned and my heart pounded and I opened my mouth and nothing came out. And yet, somehow I knew he already knew what I was going to say.

"I'm kind of inexperienced," I blurted.

"Huh?"

"I mean…I'd like to learn how to please a man, and how to be more relaxed, I guess, and I was wondering if you'd be willing to teach me."

Oh God, I wanted to die, disappear, just completely fade into oblivion. He stared at me for a moment; the look was one of delight rather than disbelief.

"You wanna be a better lover, is that it?"

"Yeah, I guess so."

"What makes you think you can't or don't please men already?"

I didn't answer him, because, quite frankly, I didn't know where to begin.

Devin scratched his head. "Hmm." I waited for his reply. He was still smiling. "No one's ever made this kind of request to me before. You want me to teach you some things, is that it?"

"Yeah, whatever there is to teach. The problem is, I can't afford to pay you. I was thinking that maybe we could do some kind of barter system, and I don't mean sex."

"I didn't think you meant that. So, what have you got to trade?"

I looked down at the cracks in the pavement, at the shade of royal purple polish that was chipping off my toenails, at the ant dragging a crumb to his condo in the concrete.

"Not much." I then looked at the used bookshop across the street, and it came to me: "I can teach you about writing. I'm very good at that."

Devin scratched his head again and let out another "Hmm." Then he said, "Why would I wanna learn how to write? It's not something I use in my career."

"Look, I can stand here all day and lecture you on the benefits of being well versed. And it's not just writing I can teach. I know all about rhetoric, theories of writing and reading, nonfiction prose...by the time we finish, I'll be a better lover and you'll be fucking Aristotle—well, not literally, of course. Look at it this way: you'll impress all your clients in academia. In fact, I'm surprised you don't know this stuff already."

"My clients don't really talk shop with me."

"Maybe they'll want to after I get through with you."

"I'm not so sure that's a selling point. The last thing my clients want to do is talk or think about work."

I was getting frustrated.

"Look, Devin. That's all I can offer you. If you're not interested, then we'll forget the whole thing. But if this is something you want to do, then this is all I know, all I'm good at."

He bent his knees slightly to meet my eye level as he leaned in, peered into my eyes, and winked. "I find that hard to believe." His tone was so sincere that I actually took a step back, as if it had swung at me. His eyes brightened. "OK, you got a deal."

I was surprised. "Good," I said coolly, "and thanks."

"I'll call you next week and we'll iron out the details of the deal. But I'm going to tell you the one stipulation that I have with all my clients: *you absolutely cannot fall in love with me.*"

"Don't flatter yourself."

With that, we parted ways once again. In my car on the way home, I compulsively tapped my ring on the steering wheel, inching along, wondering what I'd just gotten myself into with this guy who, as far as I knew, had all the morals of a tomato.

The Belt Parkway was backed up for five miles, followed by bumper-to-bumper traffic on the Long Island Expressway. When I finally got home, dinnertime was nearly over. I picked from leftovers in the fridge, watched summer reruns on TV, and went to bed.

The ceiling stared back at me nearly the entire night.

FIVE

July

Week One of the Arrangement

W E BEGAN OUR ARRANGEMENT two weeks after Independence Day, agreeing to have all of our meetings at Devin's apartment in the city because he had a less flexible schedule than I did. The arrangement was as follows: We would meet once a week for seven weeks. Each meeting would last for approximately two hours. The first hour would consist of me giving him a survey course in writing and reading nonfiction prose, much like the freshman composition course I taught at Brooklyn U; he would have weekly assignments to complete and would submit both a journal and portfolio at the final meeting. The second hour would be Devin's turn to teach me lessons in foreplay, sexual positions, methods, and orgasms. (The very words lay on the contract page like exhibitionists, flaunting prudishness at my face.) I, too, was going to have homework and complete a sort of test on our final meeting (or "a climax," as Devin cleverly dubbed it). The contract stipulated that if either of us developed "inappropriate" feelings for the other (infatuation, falling in love, or obsession) or engaged in behavior characterized as harassment, blackmail, or stalking, the contract would not only be nullified, but also a fine would be issued equivalent to the sum of total services rendered in either profession for that time period. One more thing: we were prohibited from personally socializing with each other.

We each signed our names, and Devin gave it to Christian, his partner, for notarizing and safekeeping.

The weeks leading up to the arrangement had passed in a blur. I arrived early to our first meeting filled with anticipation at the prospect of seeing Devin again, mixed with a hint of sheer terror. Devin's apartment was in West Village, a sweeping loft space with hardwood floors and a looming ceiling and soft, neutral painted walls displaying an eclectic art collection not unlike the many galleries that lined the streets of Soho. I circled the room as if I were in one of those galleries, pausing for a few moments to look at each picture. He handed me a cold bottle of Dasani water with one hand, a bottle of beer in his other. The day was hot, although the loft was air-conditioned without feeling like a freezer.

"This is quite an apartment," I remarked.

He looked around. "I like it. I got a good deal on it, right before the market went through the roof."

"You *own* this place?"

"Yeah."

"Do you get benefits with this job, too?"

He laughed. "That's cute. Shall we get started?"

For the first thirty minutes, I assigned Devin to write a narrative depicting his history of reading and writing. He sat at his laptop and poked at the keys with his index fingers while I patiently finished viewing the artwork, admiring a Warhol behind him (holy crap, a *real* Warhol!), drinking from the sweating bottle and wiping its moisture with my hand onto my leg. I then moved next to him on his suede sofa and read what was visible on the screen while he continued to type:

> When he was younger my father read all kinds of books about the history of World war I and II. He would tell me the stories when I was a kid but I wasn't interested. He also read the newspaper and liked to read the obituaries for some reason. My mother used to read to me at night before I went to bed. She read me the Cat in the Hat books and I memorized a few, like Green eggs and ham. I didn't take an interest in reading until I was older,, between 13 and 18. I read book after book and didn't stop until I got out of high school. I liked who-done-its and museum capers. I also remember learning about the beat writers and liking them a lot. I don't know hwy I stopped. The only writing I did was for school and occasionally I wrote a poem for my girlfriend.

What was his girlfriend like? I wondered. A strange kind of envy hit me like a crested wave and receded just as quickly.

When he finished, I asked him to read the entire narrative to me out loud, and he did so, fixing his typing errors along the way. We talked about the significance of the narrative and his current relationship with writing and reading.

"What do you read today?" I asked.

"The Art and Leisure section of the *Times*, mostly. I don't have time for much else."

"And what do you write?"

"Checks."

I then gave him a short piece to read called "Amid Onions and Oranges, a Boy Becomes a Man," by Donald Murray. After he finished reading it, we talked about Murray's style and use of sensory description, and the concept of writing our own story as we read someone else's. In turn, I asked him to write a response to Murray's story. Devin wrote about his first sexual encounter when he was fifteen years old. Just as he finished reading it aloud, I had turned away and took a swig of water, some of it slipping from the side of my mouth and down my chin. My cheeks were flushed, and he noticed when he looked up from the screen.

"Sorry, didn't mean to embarrass you."

"I can see you've already picked up on sensory description," I said. "That's an interesting word you chose to describe the encounter: *lascivious*. Where'd you get that word?"

"I read some sex books when I got into the business."

"You didn't mention that in your narrative."

"Didn't think that counted."

"Everything counts."

I made a mental note to look up *lascivious* when I got home.

Devin's watch beeped; the first hour was up. He then stood up and took a final swig of his beer.

"OK, Andi. Take off your shirt."

A look of horror possessed my face. "What?"

"You heard me." He picked up a remote and pressed a button, pointing it at his stereo. Club music blared from all four corners of the room. He kept pressing, and each time the speakers responded with snippets of songs, some of which I could make out the melody. My silent game of *Name That Tune* continued. "What kind of music do you like?" he asked, still station-surfing.

"Beatles, Hendrix, Clapton, Nat King Cole, Diana Krall, Norah Jones, John Mayer…"

He glared at me and cocked an eyebrow.

"I like guitars and pianos."

"What kind of music makes you feel sexy?" he asked.

I paused. "I'm not sure. I never thought about it."

"That's your first homework assignment: listen to every CD you own and make a list of songs that make you feel sexy or put you in the mood."

He walked over to the tower next to the stereo that housed his CD collection and ran his finger down the vertical façade, pulled out a case, and when he opened it, the disc slipped out and bounced and spun on the floor like an oversized coin. He picked it up like a Frisbee, and his fingerprints glossing the surface bothered me; I always held my CDs supine and by the edges. Seconds later, Etta James began to belt out "I Just Wanna Make Love to You." Devin programmed the stereo with the remote to repeat the song. He then led me to a full-length mirror.

"The first thing I want you to do is to get comfortable showing off your body in daylight. Nothing makes a guy more anxious than a woman who is constantly uptight about her body."

"Why?"

"It's like stepping into an alligator pit. If we try to say something to make the woman feel better, we ultimately say something stupid and make her feel worse; if we say nothing, that's even worse because then the woman wonders what we're thinking and fills in the answer for us, which, of course, is always the wrong one."

"What are you thinking?"

"Please don't fucking ask me if you look fat."

"What if she is, though? I mean, what if she's got layers of it and triple chins? Surely you must have clients who are both obese and insecure. What do you say to them?"

"I empower them by giving them the option to talk about it or not, or I simply start touching them and they forget about it. All they really want is to be touched, to be validated. And I've seen enough art depicting figures of every shape and size that all bodies are beautiful to me."

"You're really into art, huh?" I said, hearing the stupidity of the sentence seconds later and regretting it.

"Don't change the subject," he reprimanded. "Take off your shirt."

I stood between him and the mirror, frozen.

"Look, Andi. You agreed to trust me. I'm not going to harm you in any way, I promise. And if something is so uncomfortable that you have to stop, you can. I'll never force you to do anything you don't want to do. But if you can't even dip your feet into the water, then you might as well go home and we'll tear up the contract."

He was right; I had to start somewhere, and I had to trust him. I was wearing a heather-gray SCCC T-shirt and denim cutoffs. The straps of my white Body by Victoria bra slid off my shoulders as I tentatively pulled the tee over my head, careful not to rub it against my face and smear my makeup, most of which had gotten gooey during the stuffy subway ride. Oddly enough, a repressed memory reared its ugly head:

Fifth grade, elementary school nurse's office. Four girls and I are told to strip to our underwear for a physical. A strange, pale man with gray hair is examining us, accompanied by a nurse (also a stranger); he makes us lift our undershirts and pulls down our underpants. (Why did he do that? I can't remember.) They weigh and measure each of us and announce our numbers. I am the heaviest, and the girls make fun of me, because I am also the shortest.

Devin broke the flashback. "Nice bra. Body by Victoria. Are you wearing the matching panties?"

"No," I responded, slightly dazed. "They're blue cotton." He told me to look up at him, but I couldn't make eye contact with him. I felt his eyes looking me up and down, and I wanted to crawl out of my skin. I scanned the room for an exit.

"Tell me what you're thinking and feeling, Andi."

"I'm feeling massively uncomfortable, and thinking that I've made a huge fucking mistake to do this since I hardly know you."

"Understandable. But you had enough fucking guts to ask me in the first place. And I commend you for that. Really, I do. That's not something an inhibited woman does. Something in you wants to get past this fear and discomfort, otherwise you wouldn't be here."

My muscles relaxed slightly after he said that.

"Just listen to the music," he said. His voice lowered to a soothing pitch. He continued, "It's just you and me. No one else is in the room, no one can hurt you, and you can leave any time you want. But before you do, I want you to look in the mirror."

I turned and stood before the full-length mirror, fixated on my half-exposed body. My belly protruded from under my breasts, lifted and held by the bra. My breasts were big and saggy. My body, stocky and short. Shoulders, narrow. Back, broad. Legs, stunted. Arms, wiggly.

"What do you see?" he asked.

"Flab everywhere," I replied. "What do you see?"

"I'll bet if you stood here, completely naked and posed, you'd have a Rubenesque body. Really, Andi. You're voluptuous. You've got this fleshy belly, you're curvy, you've got ample breasts, your legs are great, and everything's in proportion."

Were we looking at the same body? I suspiciously eyed Devin's reflection in the mirror.

"*Oh, you're a smooth tawlkuh—you are, you are,*" I said in my best Marisa Tomei, *My Cousin Vinnie* impersonation. I could tell he was getting a little annoyed.

"Do I say what women want or need to hear? Yes. Is it bullshit? I don't think so. All women are beautiful, Andi. And I didn't get my reputation by bullshitting my clients. Women come back to me because I tell them the truth."

"*All* women? Oh, come on! Qualifier aside, you're a modern-day sophist! You tell them the truth, but it's a truth swaddled in words like 'voluptuous' and 'Rubenesque' and 'curvy.' Like putting Sweet'N Low in your ultra-caffeinated coffee after downing a greasy cheeseburger and fries—what difference does it make?"

"First of all, I have no idea what a sophist is. Second of all, which would you rather hear, that you're curvy and voluptuous, or that you're not as fat but your breasts are bigger than some women I've met? Truth is relative, is it not? And you just told me in my first lesson that word choice goes a long way when persuading an audience to keep reading."

My mouth hung open as I stood there. Quick fucking learner.

"It's perception. Look…" He lifted the lid on a leather ottoman next to a chair, pulled out a coffee table book, and opened it to a Reubens painting. "Do you see a fat woman? I don't. These painters regarded the female body as the essence of human life. Her flesh was life giving, her curves life affirming. And painters captured that and all its beauty."

I flipped through the book slowly, studying each earthly, heavenly figure, looking in particular at bodies that seemed to resemble my own. Why did I see these as stunning and mine as stunting?

"Go back to the mirror and look again, and tell me *one thing* you like about your body—any part."

I went back to the mirror and stood skeptically, staring at my reflection, feeling the rhythm of the song that was on its second playing. I looked at every part of my body.

"I like my eyes."

"I do too. What else?" he asked, standing behind me. I paused and looked again. "Look at your *body*."

"I like that my body seems to be flabby in proportion. It's not as if I have these little boobs and an excessive belly, or a butt that is three times the width of my waist."

He nodded while I looked some more. "I like my legs, too," I added. "They're muscular."

I looked even more and remembered how Andrew used to compliment me on my legs. My legs and my face— everything else in between was nonexistent, I guessed. Then again, I'd pretty much covered up everything else.

My observation was jarred by the touch of Devin's moist hands on my hips and waist in an attempt to move them to the music. I jumped. "*Whoa!* I forgot to tell you that I am massively ticklish."

He stepped back. "That's cute. That's really cute. We'll make that work to your advantage. In the meantime, start dancing."

Devin made me dance in front of the mirror, moving and swaying to the rhythm of the music. "*Feel* the words," he kept saying. "Don't just see yourself as half-dressed and dancing. See yourself as sumptuous."

My bra straps kept sliding off my shoulders, and my bare feet squeaked and stuck to the wood floor, knocking me off balance a couple of times. But by the fifth round of "I Just Wanna Make Love to You," I forgot that he was in the room, watching me, and instead I watched myself sway my hips and bend my knees and stick out my chest and raise my arms over my head and seductively motion to my reflection as if motioning to my lover. It never occurred to me to wonder if he was turned on while watching me.

Finally, he stopped the CD.

"Good. Your homework this week is to fall in love with your body. Actually be *attracted* to it. Also, practice dancing, because next week you're gonna dance for *me*—not the mirror—and I'm gonna have you strip further."

I made a second mental note to wear matching underwear that day.

Devin's homework was to write the first draft of a memoir, read a Patricia Hampl essay, and make a list of twenty of his favorite words. My homework was to make a list of sexy songs and dance naked in front of my mirror. I wondered who had it easier. Sitting on the hot, stuffy train packed with gray-skinned, faceless commuters, I closed my eyes and listened to Etta James in my head all the way home.

SIX

Week Two of the Arrangement

I DANCED ALL WEEK. I danced to early Duran Duran and Janet Jackson and Robert Palmer. I danced to Etta James and Ella Fitzgerald and Ray Charles. I danced to Jimi Hendrix and Joe Satriani and Stevie Ray Vaughn. I danced in my cutoffs and a bra, in bra and panties, in a bathing suit, topless, and finally, naked. I danced in daylight and in darkness. I always danced in front of the full-length mirror in my bedroom (although one early evening I caught myself checking out my reflection in a shop window). I watched the way my breasts moved, the way my arms formed shapes in the air, the way my legs jutted out, round and muscular. I watched my feet tap in rhythm. I watched my hips sway and thrust. I watched my neck turn, and strands of my hair fall in my face. I watched every curve, every curl, every roll, every muscle. And Devin was right: I fell in love with my body.

She was exquisite. I'd never seen such fullness, so much fertility in this five-foot-four-inch frame. I began to trace her, line by line, in my mind's eye: a combination of controlled contoured lines and sketchy, gestured strokes. I shadowed in the crevices where her thighs met, where the cleavage of her breast began and ended, like a waterfall. I

50

highlighted the roundness of her shoulders, the delicateness of her fingertips, the softness of her cheekbones. I posed for these portraits every day, as traces of ugliness and self-judgment melted away and beauty blossomed.

This was a far cry from the hate-hate relationship I'd had with my body ever since I was about nine and embarrassed myself one summer afternoon. Dressed in cut-off denim shorts, a child's bikini top, and Dr. Scholl's sandals, my skin a lustrous bronze from carefree play and summer vacation-swimming, I had entered the living room where my brother Joey was playing his guitar.

"Does this look sexy?" I asked, in reference to my outfit, wishing open-toed Candies shoes came in kids' sizes (for all I know, they did; but there was no way in hell my mother would have ever bought a pair for me).

He laughed. My brother *laughed* at me, and I figured I must have looked as ridiculous as I felt at that moment.

By eleven years old, I'd stopped playing outside and started reading inside—mostly novels about shy high school girl heroines winning the hearts of captains of the football team. I secretly wrote similar storylines as well. By fifteen years old, I'd discovered Drake's Ring Dings. By eighteen, I'd surrendered in defeat to the enemy that was my fat body. Even when I Slim-Fasted myself down twenty-five pounds, it didn't matter—the psychological collateral damage had already been inflicted. Since then, I'd yo-yoed the same twenty-five pounds every three or four years; I was on the upswing since I'd broken up with Andrew, plus another five pounds since my once-a-week jaunts with Maggie to the Krispy Kreme kiosk in the Brooklyn U Student Center.

———

When Devin and I met for our second meeting, he instantly noticed a difference in me.

"Wow!" he exclaimed. "You've been practicing!"

"How can you tell?"

"Your walk. You entered upright, confident. As if you own this room."

I couldn't help but reveal my enthusiasm. "It was incredible, Devin. I've never been so accepting of my body. It's such a good feeling to look in a mirror and like what I see, even if *Cosmo* is telling me I'm too many sizes too big."

"Fuck *Cosmo*—those models are all airbrushed anyway. You're real. Besides, you look gorgeous."

I blushed and turned away for a second in an attempt to hide a smile from him; I hadn't been called "gorgeous" in a long time.

"How'd you make out this week?" I asked. He raised his eyebrows and handed me three pages, typed and double-spaced, as required. One of them was the list of his twenty favorite words:

kiss	pedantic
watercolor	shaft
tarantula	lecherous
shadow	cookie
stroke	tarp
pet	canvas
cadmium	bunny
caress	didactic
lake	turpentine
ostentatious	cochlea

I read the list silently, smiling at every other word, with the exception of *tarantula.*

"What made you pick that word?" I asked, pointing to *tarantula.*

"It's just a cool-sounding word."

"And the others?"

"Mostly I either like what they are or the way they sound when they're said. The words that end in *s,* for example, can sound really sexy depending on what kind of voice you use." In a low and softened tone, almost Barry-White-ish, he cooed, "*Lecherous.*" I laughed and imitated him.

"*Carresssss,*" I exaggerated. He looked at me flirtatiously.

"Oooooo," he moaned with a wink.

Next, we talked about the Hampl essay, and the fine line between memory and imagination. What's the difference between a lie and fiction? I asked. Voice, Devin replied. Interesting answer, I thought, not to mention impressive. Finally, I read the draft of his memoir:

My fifth grade class took a field trip to the Museum of Modern Art when I was eleven years old. I didn't know anything about art, my only experiences consisted of whatever we had to do for art class in school, which was mostly paper mache projects or painting with poster paints or working with tissue paper and that sort of thing. I remember liking to finger-paint as a child, though. My mother bought me a set and for hours I set my dirty little hands into the colors and made all kinds of patterns in the newsprint.

The class went to see a Picasso exhibit. We spent a week in class learning about Picasso and all I got out of it was that he was a weird Spanish guy who was supposed to be a genius. The museum was huge. A castle of marble. Gigantic wall after gigantic wall of paintings, sculptures, drawings, and tapestries.

The class listened to the old tour guide talk about Picasso and explain the paintings, when he painted them, but I wasn't listening, and I wasn't interested in Picasso. We had passed another room that had caught my attention, and that's what I wanted to see. So I snuck away from my group and my class buddy (we always had to have a buddy when we took a field trip so as not to get lost) and went into the room. It was not as big as the other rooms, but just as well lit and quiet as the rest. I must have been a curious sight: an eleven-year-old boy dressed in Levi's jeans and a Rolling Stones glitter t-shirt and Adidas sneakers so fascinated with these pictures on the wall.

The first painting spanned almost the whole wall. It almost looked like a finger-painting, and perhaps that's what caught my attention. It had lots of blues, greens, whites, and yellows in it from far away. But when I looked up more closely, I could see just about every color you could think of in these tiny, quick brush-strokes. It was as if my eyes had suddenly become blurry and I could not make out shape or image. I circled the room and looked at other paintings and was fascinated the same way by their use of color, light, brushstrokes, and form. The dancer was my favorite. She almost looked as if she would pop right out of the painting and start twirling, just for me. She was absolutely beautiful.

I don't remember how long I was in that room, it seemed like an eternity. I don't even remember other people walking around the room. It was as if I was the only kid alive. The next thing I know, I hear someone calling my name, and it's one of my classmate's mothers who was chaperoning the field trip. She didn't yell at me but she seemed to have both a mixture of relief of having found me and anger at me for having run off. My teacher, however, had no problem yelling at me. I didn't care, though. I discovered the beauty of art that day, even though it wasn't through Picasso. I did, however, develop an appreciation for Picasso much later on, but to this day it's still the Impressionists that blow me away. I came home from the museum and announced to my parents that I was going to be an artist. My mom said, "That's nice." My dad, however, told me that the only thing that men paint is houses, and if I wanted to be an artist the first thing I should paint was a pair of fairy wings for myself. I never could stand his closemindedness.

"I didn't really know how to end it," he said, almost apologetically.

I read through the draft once, and then a second time, taking out my felt-tip blue pen and making notes in the margins, underlining some phrases and circling certain words. Devin watched me do all this, and with my peripheral vision I saw his apprehension. The writing was choppy and repetitive in style and structure, as well as laced with comma splices, with dabblings in metaphor and description; much like my freshman students' first drafts. And yet, I saw something else here, something more complex bubbling underneath the surface. I see that with all student writing—the possibility that lives within the flaws.

"What do you like about this draft?" I asked him, breaking the silence. Puzzled by the question, he studied the words as if they were cryptic markings, as if the idea of liking his writing was something foreign to him.

"Actually, what I like is what I didn't really write about. It wasn't just that I fell in love with those paintings, but that I also found them on my own. No tour guides, no teachers. It was the *solitude* of the moment—I was in my own world, and it could've lasted ten minutes or two hours, I really don't know. And maybe there was a little excitement at having escaped from the herd, so to speak."

"That's what I see," I responded. "There's so much in this memoir that's not on the page yet. So much you can do with it."

We discussed figures of speech and adding description and letting the moment of revelation—the discovery of beauty, both in art and solitude, and the rejection of his father—show itself without him having to tell his readers. As time ran out, Devin looked at me with admiration.

"Wow. You're really good at this."

"Thanks."

I must have sounded unconvinced by his sincerity, because he continued. "No, I mean it. You really know how to see what's going on while giving constructive criticism at the same time. I think I was expecting you to tell me it was crap. If I had a teacher like you the first time around, I might have remembered more about writing. Hell, I might even not have been so bad at it."

"Well, you're not a bad writer; actually, I think this is quite good. You're inexperienced, that's all."

"Same as you."

"Huh?"

"There's a ravenous, sexy lover in you, and we're gonna bring her out just like you're gonna help me with my writing. You'll see."

He was so corny that I gagged in the process of laughing and swallowing at the same time. I took a sip of water. Devin looked unfazed.

"OK," he said, standing up. "Your turn. Strip."

My eyes widened and I coughed again as I looked at him.

"Geez, you could be a little more tactful. Whatever happened to foreplay?"

"First of all, foreplay is next week. Second of all, I don't wanna be tactful. Tactful is '*Now take off all your clothes, piece by piece, and don't worry, your body is beautiful,*'" he said in a condescending voice. "We did that last week. You're beyond that now. Let it out."

"How much am I letting out?"

"As much as you can."

"Would you at least lower the blinds so I'm not giving the rest of the city a free show?"

He rolled his eyes and closed the blinds, shutting out the streams of sunlight that cascaded onto the walls and floor and sofa. I noticed the color of the sofa had changed from a slightly off-white to taupe once the rays were extinguished. He liked neutrals.

This time I wore a matching pink bra and panties, again by Victoria's Secret. Beads of sweat formed at my temples and rolled down my flushed face. He took a step towards me, and I backed away. "What are you gonna do?" I asked.

"Relax. Geez, Andi. You gotta trust me."

I remembered:

I am twenty years old and in one of the coed fitting rooms at the Gap. An eighteen-year-old employee accidentally unlocks my room for another customer and gets an eyeful of me in bra and panties and one leg in a pair of size twelve jeans that are too tight. I recoil in both surprise and horror and don't know what to cover first. He promptly but disingenuously apologizes and slams the door, and I am mortified. When I finish changing, I bring the tight jeans and other rejects to the entrance of the fitting rooms and hand him the stuff without making eye contact. As I walk away, the tow-headed kid mutters under his breath but loud enough for me to hear, "Get over yourself, bitch; there was nothing worth looking at."

"Fuck you, Devin." The words fired out of my mouth like a bullet. "You take your clothes off. You think this is easy? I don't even *know* you." I recalled saying that to him once before.

Devin didn't even flinch at my words; instead, he did as I commanded and started to remove his T-shirt and jeans, revealing a chiseled body and navy blue silk boxer shorts. The hair on his chest was dark and short and drew a line from his breastbone to his navel. His skin was tan and firm, his muscles toned and trimmed without bulging or looking like an abs infomercial. His legs were powerful and sturdy and tall. I was viewing a replica of Michelangelo's *David*. He stood before me, completely uninhibited, and stretched his arms out, almost in a Christ-like way. My mouth hung open like a thirsty dog.

"See how easy it can be?" he said.

I had to catch my breath before I spoke again. "Of course it's easy for *you*—look at you! Who wouldn't wanna show off a body like that?"

"Andi, you just got through telling me that you fell in love with your body."

"Yeah, well, that moment's over."

"Why?"

I didn't answer him.

Devin looked at me with compassion, then closed the rest of the shades in the room. Next, he turned on the stereo and went through his CD collection. "We've had enough of Etta James," he said, more to himself than me. He finally settled on a Latin album. The syncopated drums were no match for the rhythm or the rate my heart was beating at. He padded back towards me, his bare feet making light thumping sounds on the hardwood floor, and stood right in front of me, invading my space. I felt myself lean back slightly. His eyes locked into mine and overpowered me in such a way that my insecurities were stopped in their tracks by stun rays shooting out of his pupils. And yet, his sienna irises radiated firm gentleness, as if to protect the rest of me from freezing in fear.

"OK. It's just you and me and the music. No one can see us, and no one else is here. Pretend you're fully dressed. Do you like the music?"

I nodded.

"Good," he said. Let's dance."

The sweaty soles of my feet stuck to the floor. Devin tried again, patiently, without coaxing. "You can't please a man until you please yourself. Men like women who like their bodies, who feel comfortable in their own skin."

"I never met such a man. I've only met men who like women with bodies that would make Barbie wanna throw on a pair of sweats."

"Then you've been meeting the wrong men. Close your eyes. Pretend you're in your bedroom." He leaned closer and whispered, "No one can *judge* you, Andi, and no one *will*."

How did he know?

I began to sway to the music, and when I opened my eyes, I looked up and met his smile. I smiled back and moved even more. He began dancing too, and within minutes we were bathing in the bossa nova beats, twirling and twisting and tapping. The two of us—an escort and a writing professor—dancing in our underwear in broad daylight on a hardwood floor in a loft on the West Side. All fear flew away; I felt free and light. When the music slowed down to a ballad, Devin extended his hand to me. "Wanna?" he asked. I took his hands and pressed myself close to him, anxiety creeping back in.

"I haven't done this in a while," I confessed. *Not since Andrew and I danced at our friend Marcy's wedding two years ago, when he held me close and blew in my ear and looked into my eyes and told me he loved me, told me that the next time we danced it'd be at our own wedding...*

"I mean, slow danced with a guy—not danced in my underwear in broad daylight. I've never done that."

He noted, "You're going to be doing a lot of 'firsts' from now on."

Hell yeah.

We circled the floor awkwardly a few times, and then fell into rhythm. Devin held my hand as if it were porcelain, while resting his other hand on my back in the same ginger manner. His skin was surprisingly smooth, and his scent was overpowering—no manufactured cologne could ever smell as good, I thought. I imagined someone trying, though: "Introducing Giorgio Armani's *Devin...*" My sweat turned to chills running from my feet up the backs of my legs and converging up my spine to my neck. I bravely decided to make eye contact—God, his eyes were so compassionate, so nonjudgmental, so *honest*. The chills turned into tingling, and I completely forgot we were both stripped down.

I wanted to kiss him.

The music stopped, and I could tell that he sensed my impulse. He let go of me and took a step back.

"You're gonna have to beat the men off with a stick," he said.

I said nothing, motionless.

"You can put your clothes back on now."

He snapped one of the shades open, and it flapped wildly as the sun burst in and blinded me out of my daze. I put my knee-length denim skirt on first, followed by a soft red blouse. He also dressed.

"You know, you really do have a nice body. You should show it off more. And you look really good in red."

This time, I believed him.

That was my homework assignment: show off my body. His was to start keeping a journal, choose three paragraphs of his memoir to revise, and read an article called "Closing My Eyes as I Speak: An Argument for Ignoring Audience" by Peter Elbow ("the Paul McCartney of rhetoric and composition," I call him) in addition to two memoirs: one by Annie Dillard and the other by Stephen King.

That evening, I went clothes shopping at the Roosevelt Field Mall and purchased two low-cut, scoop-neck tees with cami sleeves (a 2-for-$10 sale), one red and one periwinkle; and a short, sleek, linen skirt that flattened my tummy without straightening out my hips. I also bought a pair of espadrilles (another sale) with a two-and-a-half-inch heel. As I passed the Gap on my way out, I spied a teenage boy with red hair folding shirts in front of a display table, who looked up at me for a moment and then resumed his folding, and I strutted all the way back to my car.

SEVEN

Week Three of the Arrangement

O N T H E D A Y of our third visit, I took off my sandals and curled up on Devin's sofa as if I lived there myself, surprised by my sudden gesture of comfort and familiarity. Devin didn't seem to mind, however.

"So," I began, "tell me about your weekend."

He eyed me suspiciously. "You don't wanna look at my memoir? I revised more than three paragraphs."

"We'll get to that. First, tell me about your weekend. Rather, read to me."

He opened his laptop and read bits and pieces from his journal, mostly about the dates he was on, describing the women—he was quite descriptive of the women—and where they went.

"OK. Now I want you to rewrite what you just read to me, only I want you to pretend you are writing a letter to your mother."

It was his turn to look at me with wide eyes and a dropped jaw. He stared at the screen for a few seconds, then started and stopped several times, feverishly back-spacing or deleting. Meanwhile, I read his revised memoir, making notes in the margins. Finally, out of frustration, he stopped and revealed a look of surrender, diverting my attention from his draft to him.

"What," I said like a statement more than a question.

"Why am I writing my mother a letter about what I did over the weekend?"

"Because she lives across the country and you haven't written or spoken to her in a while. You want to give her an idea of how you're living your life."

"First of all, my mother lives in Massapequa. Second of all, she wants to know nothing of my life—at least not *this* part of my life. Third of all, for what purpose would I—"

"*A-ha!*" I interrupted. "You said the magic word: *purpose*. Audience and purpose are inextricably linked. You write a cover letter with the purpose of getting an interview. You write a shopping list with the purpose of remembering what you need to buy, or giving the list to whoever's doing the shopping. You write a memoir for the purpose of recreating a memory or event to convey a new meaning for the reader, even if that reader is you. And each of these things takes place in a different context, be it the personal, daily life, the workplace, et cetera. If you are uncertain about your purpose, then your audience is ambiguous. If you are uncertain about your audience, then your writing is ambiguous."

"Makes sense."

"For example, what's the purpose of your journal?"

"I wrote it because you told me to."

"And the audience?"

He paused and thought for a second.

"You know, I just realized, I knew you were going to read it, so I had you in mind most of the time."

"How did that influence what you wrote?"

"Not so much what I wrote, but the way I wrote it. I thought a lot about the description and imagery. There were even times I felt like I was talking to you."

"And if you were writing for a magazine…say, a profile piece: 'A Day in the Life of an Escort'—how would you write that?"

"Depends on the magazine: *Reader's Digest*, or *Cosmo*?"

"You get the gist," I said, smiling and pointing at him.

He grinned proudly.

"I liked what Peter Elbow said about the idea that sometimes you've got to ignore your audience, and doing so can lead to better writing," he said as he flipped a page of the photocopied article until he found a passage that he'd underlined, and then read directly from it: "*As writers, then, we need to learn when to think about audience and when to put readers out of mind.*"

"Yes," I concurred.

"I had a hard time with the section in which he defended the claim that sometimes the audience is an audience of one: the self."

"Actually, I think he's responding to the claim that there's no such thing as private discourse, or no audience at all. And yet, I think both claims hold some truth. For example, in the film *Imagine*, John Lennon is trying to talk an obsessed fan back to reality. He basically tells the kid that the songs he wrote were for himself and no one else."

"Wow. I never thought of that."

"The kid had a hard time with it, too. When he asked Lennon what he meant by 'you're gonna carry that weight,' Lennon wryly answered, 'That was Paul's tune. You'll have to ask him.'"

Devin grinned again, and I continued, "*The Simpsons* writers, the writers for the classic Bugs Bunny cartoons, all confessed to writing for themselves. That's why they're so damn funny. In such cases, you can tell when a writer stops writing for him- or herself and starts trying to meet the expectations of an audience, especially when some executive asshole claims to know better. The show tanks as a result."

"So did McCartney," he added.

"But what if Lennon wrote songs that he didn't play for anyone or put on tape? What about the scripts that went into the fire without anyone's viewing? That's what Elbow means by private discourse. In those cases, you ignore all conventions of audience awareness, *including* the audience of self."

"Cool."

We then moved on to the other memoirs. "Why these two?" he asked. "What do they have in common?"

I responded, "Annie Dillard and Stephen King couldn't be more far apart in terms of genre and style. In those aspects, it's as if they come from different worlds. And yet, they speak the same language—that is to say, they know language so well, and use it the way a good painter uses light and color and form."

His eyes brightened at my art analogy. As we analyzed each memoir's content and language, we talked about ways Devin could use language to convey his meaning in his own memoir.

"I could use words that keep a reader interested. Not just for the sake of being smart or literary, but to make them feel like they're in that museum gallery with me."

"Very good," I said. "Make them feel what you want them to feel. You have absolute power, Devin. Other writers or teachers or readers can guide you, give you feedback, tell you what they like or don't like; but ultimately, it's your story and your truth."

"Wow," he said. "I had no idea."

"No idea what?"

"That I could do such a thing. I mean, I know writing has power. I guess I never thought of myself having access to it."

"Why wouldn't you?" I asked. He pondered this.

"I don't know." He grinned. "But I'm glad that I do."

Devin closed his laptop. Time was up.

"So," he began, "tell me about *your* weekend. I see you went shopping. Nice espadrilles, by the way." He winked.

I stuck out my ankle and proudly showed off my shoe, my toenails painted a deep red. He then switched the conversation. "Now it's *your* turn to do some freewriting."

I looked at him and raised my eyebrows.

"Make a list of what gets you in the mood," he instructed.

My back stiffened and my stomach tightened. He noticed this and rolled his eyes. "Here we go again," he said.

"Didn't we already cover this?" I said.

"When?"

"That day at Junior's."

"Andi, if you can't *talk* about good sex, how can you *have* good sex?"

I could've debated this point, but I kept my mouth shut and stared at my notepad instead. Like Devin, I struggled with what should have been a relatively easy assignment. After about five minutes, I only had three things on my list:

- having my neck (and pulse points) kissed
- having my feet rubbed
- Nat King Cole ballads

He made me read the list aloud, and I felt the spark of his eyes burning through the page and stinging my skin.

"Cute," he said.

"*Cute?*" I asked, insulted.

"Yeah. That's it?"

I looked at him sheepishly. "Actually, Devin, I never gave it much thought."

"How come?"

"I don't know. I guess I was always so self-conscious about whether I was doing it right or wrong that I never considered what I liked or disliked."

"OK. Then tell me what you do to get the guy in the mood."

Again, I paused. "I don't know," I said after some thought.

He stood up and took off his shirt, and like last time, a flash of heat ran up my spine. "Pretend I'm your lover," he said.

Pretend? Woof.

"Touch me the way you'd touch him. Come on to me the way you'd come on to him. Do everything but kiss me."

"But what if kissing is one of the things I do?"

"I just don't want you to get carried away."

I looked at the floor in an attempt to hide my disappointment. "OK." Then I hesitated. "Don't you think you should teach me how to kiss?" I asked.

He cracked a grin that mixed modesty with mischief. "You don't need to learn how to kiss."

"How do you know? You've never kissed me."

"I don't need to kiss you to know that kissing's not your problem."

"What is my problem?"

"Your problem is that you *think* you're a bad kisser; you *think* you're a bad lover. You think too much. Just *do* it, Andi. Be a good kisser. Be a good lover."

"Ha. Easy for you to say."

"Easy to do, too."

"Then what do I need you for?" I asked. Sarcasm aside, it was a good question, I thought. And I wanted him to answer it.

"You're so good at avoidance," he said. "You're supposed to be showing me how you get your guy in the mood."

I frowned, irked by his assertion. But rather than fuel his claim and further avoid the task by arguing the point with him, I stood and slowly approached him, feeling silly in this role-playing mode. He was six foot two, and the two and a half inches on my shoes helped me reach up and run my fingers through his hair. It was short and full and silky and layered, and I moved even closer. He followed my hand as it moved through his hair by putting his own hand on my arm.

"I used to do this with Andrew," I said softly, in almost a whisper.

"Who's Andrew?" he replied in the same quiet tone. It suddenly occurred to me that I'd never mentioned him.

"My ex-fiancé."

"No kidding. I didn't know you had a fiancé."

"Well, I did."

"And his name was Andrew?"

"Yep."

"Did people ever call you Andy and Andi?"

"You think you're the first jackass to think that's funny or original?"

"Well, did they?"

"He's always 'Andrew.'"

"Not *Drew*?"

"Good God, no. I picture guys named Drew wearing argyle sweaters and Dockers and loafers."

"When'd you break up?"

"About a year and a half ago."

"Is that why you moved back to New York?"

I didn't answer. Instead, I caressed his face, now cupping it with both hands, and then followed my fingers along his neck and down his bare chest. His skin was firm, his muscles tight, his arms full and massive. God, I wanted to kiss him. As I moved my hands back up to his shoulders and massaged them almost like kneading bread, my nails slightly digging into his skin, he grabbed me by the wrists.

"OK, that's good enough," he said. I looked in his eyes, but quickly turned my attention to his hands, which now took hold of my own and squeezed them—I couldn't tell which of us was trembling. He took a breath, as if to compose himself.

"Wanna know what I think?"

"What." My breathing slowed down.

"I think you're doing what you want a man to do to you, and you don't even realize it. I think you'd like someone to, for instance, touch your hair..." he tucked a strand of my hair behind my left ear, "to run his fingers along your neck..." the back of his hand glided over my left carotid, along the edge of my chin, and down the center of my neck, stopping at my cleavage, like a melting ice cube, "to just completely saturate you with touch..." he whispered in my ear.

I closed my eyes and my breathing deepened. When his index finger barely grazed my left breast, I let out a soft sigh that turned into a moan, and fell into him. He caught me just as I snapped out of his sexual trance. Once again, his eyes burned into me.

"Can I have some ice water?" I asked foggily, still staring at him. He commanded me to sit on the sofa and got me a bottle of Dasani and a glass of wine for himself. He then sat next to me. After a few sips, he began talking.

"It's all about communication," he said. "You wanna let him know what you like, and find out what he likes. And like readers, each one is different. What one does well, another may suck at—forgive the pun. One guy may like when you run your fingers through his hair, while another may want you to run them someplace else. Lovers aren't mind readers, Andi. Never assume he knows what you want—you gotta tell him. And trust me: he'll want to know. He'll feel good knowing he's making you feel good. Men feel a sense of satisfaction when they can make a woman come, 'cause they don't know what the hell's goin' on in there. And he'll be more willing to tell you what he likes."

"But what if I don't like to do what he wants me to do, or what he likes? Or what if I don't like what he likes to do?"

"Well, then, he might not be the right guy for you."

I looked at him, confused. "Just because we don't agree on foreplay?"

"Depends on how important it is to him, or to you."

I pondered this and sipped my water.

"Isn't it true that most men would rather skip the foreplay?" I asked.

"Not if it's the best part of the sex."

"I thought the other part was supposed to be the best part. You know, the 'biggie.'"

He leaned in close, and I could still feel the heat coming off his body from our role-playing before. "Let me tell you a little secret, Andi."

"I was hoping you'd kiss me instead."

"Everything they told you about sex is wrong," he practically whispered.

"Who is 'they'?" I whispered back.

"Whoever told you what you think you know." He then leaned back on the sofa and looked at me more quizzically. "How *did* you learn about sex?"

No one had ever asked me this, and I'd never really given it much thought. I grew up in an Italian, patriarchal household on the North Shore of Long Island, the youngest of three. My two brothers, Joseph and Anthony, were handsome, popular, and extremely talented musicians, both playing professionally by the time they were adolescents. Joey was a jazz pianist; Tony, a rock guitarist. They were quite protective of me until they moved out and went on the road with their respective bands. They would beat up bullies and each would walk on the other side of me, like bodyguards, regardless of whether we went to the mall or the movies. I certainly didn't turn to them for sex education. Whenever I went to one of the seamier dives where they performed, they would actually announce to the audience that I was their little sister and "off-limits," much to my embarrassment. In sixth grade, when Gary Whitmore sent me a Valentine along with his phone number and a picture of himself, Tony called Gary and warned him to "stay the hell away" from me. The next day, Gary stopped speaking to me; the week after that, he gave my friend Rosie a little stuffed bear.

I don't remember much about my father; he died from a heart attack shortly after my thirteenth birthday. He worked a lot and played golf and guitar on Saturdays and attended church on Sundays with the rest of the family. He forbade me to watch soap operas ("those things are disgusting"), wear two-piece bathing suits ("you're not a woman; you're just a girl"), and swearing was absolutely forbidden in the house, dammit. After my father died, my mother was too consumed with grief to usher her daughter through any pubescent curiosities. And the older I got, the more she seemed to resent me for my youth and vitality and figure. She criticized every accessory I wore, and the sound of my laugh was "too suggestive."

She bought me baggy sweaters and spandex leggings. By the junior prom, I had gained thirty pounds and the boys reviled me and gawked at the Heather Locklear types instead.

Public school treated the matter of sex education like something as rote and sterile as the SATs, and I was simply too scared to ask my friends, one of whom called me a prude after I refused to look at the *Playgirl* magazine she had managed to get her hands on.

I babbled all this to Devin, barely pausing for a breath. So then, how did I learn about sex?

"Judy Blume books, I guess," I finally answered.

"Trust me, there are better sources."

My head sank; God, how pathetic. I'd felt this feeling before. Shame penetrated every internal organ like bile, churning and eating away from the inside out.

Despite telling me that lovers aren't mind readers, Devin responded to my thoughts as if I'd spoken them out loud.

"What are you so ashamed of?"

My head stayed tilted toward the floor, and I took a few seconds to find a voice with which to answer him. "My inexperience."

"I don't think that's anything to be ashamed of. At least you're learning something now. You're willing to own your experience. And besides, it's not like you had much encouragement growing up."

"What do you mean?"

"I mean, you were told that you were off-limits, and that sex was some big taboo, a secret, and you were not worthy to know about it."

I had never realized that. Suddenly I saw my childhood through new lenses.

"And that's a bum rap," he continued. "It's bad enough that society teaches us that a woman's body is supposed to be a thing of service. You had a double-edged sword. Your brothers, although well meaning, sent a message that you were to serve no one. And both notions are dead wrong. They punished you for being who you were, for being attractive to and pursued by others. They probably thought you were too good for the average guy, but you took it to mean that *you* were the one who wasn't good enough. I'll bet you were vivacious and even sexy as a girl, and your family snuffed that right out of you."

He reached out, gently touched my chin with his hand, and lifted it, to find tears streaming down my cheek. He moved his hand from my chin and smudged the wet line across my face. I tried to look at him, but couldn't.

"You're a very sexy woman, do you know that?"

I shook my head.

"You wanna know something else?" he asked.

I felt like a little girl, and he was soothing away a scrape on my knee or exonerating me for the vase I broke. "What," I nearly whimpered.

"You turned me on before."

I sat up a bit.

"Really?"

"Hell yeah."

"How? What did you like?"

"I liked the way you stroked my hair. It's been a while since a woman's done that to me." He took my hand and held it, touching each finger. "I like the feel of your hands.

You've got these delicate fingers. I'll bet men like your gentleness."

If they did, they never told me.

I looked at his hand and moved my own so that his was now in mine.

"I like hair that I can run my fingers through," I said, looking at his dark brown layers. "I like *your* hair."

Womanhood rushed back in and took over, and my voice lowered to a soft, round tone. "And I loved the way your hands felt on my neck," I added.

He smiled and looked down—I could swear he was blushing. I moved close enough so that our legs were touching, and leaned in to him. "Do you want more?" I asked. He laughed lightly and very slightly moved back, and I recoiled in secret mortification when I assumed that he thought I was kidding.

"So," I began, sitting straight up, recomposing myself and resuming a scholarly voice, "is the purpose of foreplay to have better intercourse?"

"Depends on your audience," he said with a wink. "Actually, I think the purpose of foreplay should be pleasure, plain and simple. Stop worrying about it so much and the intercourse stuff will take care of itself."

"Again with the pleasure—you're a hedonist, you know that?"

"It's my job," he said earnestly.

"Are you saying that your clients enjoy the foreplay more than the actual sex?"

"That *is* the sex."

"What do you mean?"

"I don't go all the way with my clients, Andi."

If I had a dollar for every jaw-dropping moment with Devin, I could've bought his friggin' loft.

"*You don't?*"

"Didn't you read the contract?"

"But you're *an escort!* What are they paying you all that money for?"

"To please them."

"And you do that without actually…"

"Inserting my penis?"

The words made me wince.

"There are lots of ways to get laid, Andi. In fact, most female orgasms don't happen during intercourse."

"Actually, that I knew."

"Have you ever had an orgasm?"

"Yes and no." Despite my hope that the conversation would end there, he was clearly waiting for me to continue. "I never had one with a man. I mean—"

"You mean, you did it yourself?"

"Yeah," I said squeamishly.

"That's pretty common. So, how did the men you were with react when you didn't have one with them?"

"Well, my first boyfriend took it personally that he couldn't get me to have one, so after that I started faking it."

"You faked all your orgasms?"

"Yeah—that I've got experience in."

"How'd you learn to do it?"

"Movies."

"Porn or regular?"

"Geez, are you kidding me? Regular."

He laughed. "I know, I just wanted to mess with you. So what kind of orgasm do you give yourself? I mean, how do you do it?"

My face burned a bright red. "I can't."

"You can't what?"

"I can't tell you."

"OK. Last question on the subject: clitoral or vaginal?"

Oh good God. My face buried in my hands, I had to reach deep to find the guts to answer. "The first one." Finally, I detoured the questioning. "So then, what do *you* do?"

"I do lots of things with my clients, except, you know…" Rather than use words, he made a fist and moved it back and forth in a push-pull motion. "…and none have walked away dissatisfied. Well, few…I mean, they know ahead of time what they will or won't get from me, and they keep coming—forgive the pun—to see me, that is, so obviously it's enough for them. They love it, actually. For once, they don't have to work so hard, don't have to literally bend over backwards to please the guy, after which he rolls over and goes to sleep, leaving her feeling all alone. I told you: it's not about me; it's about them."

"Are all the escorts you employ like that?"

"Not all. Christian used to be, but he stopped servicing his clients altogether. He manages the business now."

"How come? I mean, how come he stopped?"

"He wanted a serious relationship."

"And?"

"And women are much more tolerant when they find out you're not actually doin' it." He continued, "James stopped, except with a few regular clients, and Simon still does even after we told him not to. Both of them charge extra and pocket the cash—that way, if they get arrested, Christian and I can say that we had no knowledge and can produce their contracts, which state that they're not supposed to."

"Smart thinking. And you?"

"What about me?"

"You don't?"

"Nope."

"Never did?"

"I told you—in my experience, that's not what my clients need."

"It's what *I* need," I blurted in frustration, surprised I'd said the words out loud.

"Oh, you definitely need to get laid," he agreed. "When was the last time you did?"

Again, I pondered. How could I answer that question truthfully? I thought about the last time Andrew and I were together, in a bed-and-breakfast inn on the Cape, the night he told me about Tanya. It was supposed to be the night we finally "did it." Flowers, candles, and expectations in abundance. We'd been engaged for four months...

We undress each other, and he lowers me on the bed, soft acoustic guitar music playing in the background. He touches me in all the places I love to be touched: up my thigh, inside my elbow, behind my earlobe. I run my fingers through his long hair and feel my body tremble. We're both naked. Just as he's about to go inside, I sit up, overly apologetic. He stares at me coldly for a long second, and then proclaims, "That's it."

"Please," I plead. "I just need more time. I can do this. I want to. I'm just not ready yet." I slip my robe on and quickly cover up.

"When, Cutch? When will you be ready? It's been almost a year."

"I don't know," I cry.

"What is wrong with you?"

"I don't know...I just can't. It doesn't feel right. Maybe if we wait till we're married. Maybe it would be more special then."

"Then what? You'll freeze up on our wedding night? No, honey. I'm sorry. I know I said I'd wait for you, but I can't anymore. In fact..." He hesitates. "I wasn't going to tell you this, but there's someone else. A friend of mine named Tanya from the writers' group."

I feel the life force energy drain from my body.

"I was with her once, but told her I was in love with you. But now, she's fallen in love with me, and I told her I would let her know how things went this weekend."

"Are you telling me that you're testing me this weekend to see if I'll be a good enough lover so you can break up with your other lover?"

"Cutch, you have to understand. She doesn't have any issues, and she's more than ready. You can't ask me to wait for you anymore."

"I never asked you; you promised me on your own. Are you in love with her?"

He waits for a moment, then looks me in the eye. "I think so. Look, I would've been content to stay with you—"

"CONTENT?"

"—but this sex thing is really a problem for me. You just don't satisfy me, and your company isn't enough. I'm sorry. I don't mean to hurt your feelings."

I am too numb to be angry. I feel as if I've shrunk to the size of a stain on the carpet. "You can take me home now," I say. I robotically walk to the bathroom, change, and hastily pack my bags...

"At least a year and a half ago, when Andrew and I were still together. Maybe longer," I lied.

"No kidding. So why'd you break up?"

"He decided to marry someone else." I looked down at the floor, avoiding Devin's eyes.

"I'm sorry to hear that," he replied, the tone of his voice softening. He took a sip of wine. "That's it?"

"What do you mean, 'that's it'? Isn't that enough?"

"Didn't he give you a reason as to why he chose this other woman?"

"Are you implying that it was *my* fault?"

He held up his hands as if to deflect a punch. "Whoa— *chill out!* I wasn't impl—I was just asking a question."

"Why?"

"Look, I'm just trying to get to know you, that's all. You asked me to be your teacher. I need to find out what you need to learn. Don't you do the same thing with your students—assess their needs?"

This guy was really starting to piss me off by throwing everything back into my face. I stood up and took the water bottle with me.

"Maybe we should forget this whole deal," I said. Devin stood up, too.

"I don't think we should. I think you really need it. And besides," he said, pointing to the laptop, "I'm liking this. I'm actually learning something."

I looked at the laptop on the cedar coffee table. Somehow, it just didn't feel like an even trade. He was getting off way too easy, in more ways than one.

"Is this what you do?" he asked, moving in close to me. "Do you quit when it gets hard?"

"Do *you*?" I retorted, looking down at his crotch and then back into his eyes, nodding my head in the direction of where we were standing during our contrived foreplay session. Frankly, my boldness surprised me, and him too, because his back stiffened and he looked away from me.

"Time's up," he said coldly.

EIGHT

Week Four of the Arrangement

S UNDAY AFTERNOON, two days before my fourth
meeting with Devin, Maggie and I weaved between
racks of sportswear at Express in the Roosevelt Field Mall.
Clothes shopping was typically a nightmare for both of
us—I needed petite-plus sizes while she needed tall sizes
and had trouble fitting blouses across her back and chest.
And jeans? Forget it. A more humane form of torture
would be to tie me to a chair while every woman in a size
four lined up to say mean things to me.

"So? You've not said one word to me about your latest
class with Devin the escort."

"Shhhh," I said. Maggie didn't exactly have an "inside
voice." "And they're not 'classes,' Mags. They're...it's an
arrangement."

"Everything go OK?"

"It was fine."

She knew better, but didn't press me. So far, I'd been
pretty detailed about what went on at the first couple of
meetings, but I'd said nothing about what happened at
the last one. Instead, she watched me pull out sleeveless
camisoles and short skirts and hold them up to me in
front of a nearby full-length mirror.

"You're getting daring," she said of my clothing choices. "So what've you learned so far?"

"That I've got a lot more to learn."

"What are you teaching him?"

"We just finished Elbow's 'Closing My Eyes,' and this week we're moving on to David Bartholomae."

Maggie raised her eyebrows and opened her mouth. "*Bartholomae*? Geez, Andi, he's not getting a PhD! Isn't there something a little more racy?"

I shushed her again.

"The deal was that I teach him about writing and rhetoric, and he teaches me...what he knows."

"What's he writing?"

"A memoir about his first museum trip when he was a kid. He's actually a pretty good writer. He's got a flair for description. He just needs to practice and season it a little, you know?"

"Whatever you say," she said.

"What's that supposed to mean?" I asked.

"It just seems to me that you're squandering a golden opportunity."

"To do what?"

"I don't know—to dig deeper or something. Geez, Andi, you've got him reading *Bartholomae*!"

"That was the deal, though. I'm teaching him what I know, same as him. And he seems to be into it. At least that's what he tells me."

"Well, fine then. I guess you know what you're doing."

Maggie did nothing to boost my self-confidence; I wound up spending the rest of the day second-guessing my lesson plans, and composed numerous variations of letters, phone calls, and face-to-face confrontations of calling the whole arrangement off, acting on none of them.

———————

I found myself looking forward to my meetings with Devin the way kids looked forward to going to an amusement park or their best friend's built-in pool on hot summer days. When we met at our usual time on Tuesday, Devin was his usual professional self, and neither of us said anything about the way things had ended the last time.

This time we switched turns and my instruction came first. Devin had me do figure drawings of two nude models, one male and one female, that he hired for the hour. Having not taken an art class since high school, and having never worked with models clad in anything less than cut-up sweatshirts, scrunchy socks, and acid-washed jeans that zippered down the ankles, my sketches were tight and stiff. The exception, of course, was the genital areas, which I practically ignored altogether. Devin watched over my shoulder for the first couple of drawings (which made me even more uncomfortable than the naked models did), then ripped the newsprint out of the pad and made me start over on a clean sheet, this time focusing solely on those neglected areas. The models seemed undisturbed by his instruction, even when he adjusted their poses and the lighting. How did they do it? I wondered. Stand there in the middle of the room, frozen in pose, watching me hone in on them?

Midway through the fourth sketch, I started to use the gummy eraser and other drawing tools Devin provided me, and my eyes shifted less apprehensively from model to newsprint.

By the seventh drawing, he nodded in approval. "Better," he said. "You're loosening up."

"Thanks," I said.

"Whaddya think?"

"Of what?"

"Of your work?"

"I don't think I'm flattering them much."

"Ever seen a naked body this close up before?"

I remembered the time my friend Candace stole a *Playgirl* from the drugstore she worked for in high school:

At first I refuse to look at it, and she calls me a prude. To prove her wrong, I take it home for a week to "study." I spend an hour with it and then hide it under my bed for the rest of the week. When I give it back, Candace calls me a prude yet again because I refuse to show her my "favorite" picture.

"Sort of," I answered.

Why I didn't just lie and show any ol' picture to Candace, I don't know. Perhaps I lacked confidence in my faking it abilities and was afraid of picking the "wrong" one. I had thought myself some kind of weirdo back then—not because I was looking at these muscular men and their appendages, but because I wasn't turned on by them. The pinups of guys like Sting or Jon Bon Jovi, shirtless and in tight leather pants, were much more appealing and provocative. It seemed that the less I saw, the more I liked. And that trend had continued for the next fifteen years or so.

After I scrutinized bodies and wrestled with charcoal-based crayon and newsprint paper, Devin scrutinized and wrestled with various texts. We had moved from reading Peter Elbow articles to scholars David Bartholomae and Kenneth Burke, who, among others, argue a theory that claims all writing, even personal, is constructed from previous texts and writers and social influences. Thus, writing, reading, and even teaching are social acts.

"Art follows this same logic," Devin proposed. I didn't debate him.

We freewrote and talked about lessons we learned in school (both in and out of the classroom), family mottoes, and regional dialects or word distinctions (people in Massachusetts call a water fountain a "bubbla"; upstate New Yorkers call soda "pop"), exploring language and style as a product of those contexts. Devin especially liked my New England pronunciation of "Foll Riv-ah" as opposed to the brusque Long Island "Fawl Rivuh."

"In other words, we're not just bringing our own interpretation to a text, but our upbringing, religious teaching, political persuasion, et cetera," he said.

"You know, you would make a good composition teacher, Devin. You really get this stuff."

He offered a humble smile. "Really?" He seemed touched by my compliment.

I returned his smile but bashfully looked away.

———

Two days later, Devin called me at home in the morning. Just out of the shower, I raced to catch the phone before the machine picked up, my towel slipping off. With one hand on the towel and another on the receiver, I answered with a hurried, "Hello?"

"Hey," he said, "it's me." As if we'd known each other for ages.

"Hi." My heart leapt into my throat. "What's up?"

"Nothing much."

An awkward silence passed through like a subway train.

"Did you have a question about this week's homework assignment?" I asked as my hair dripped water beads down the phone and onto the rug.

"Oh, uh, no." He paused. "I was just wondering, are you free this afternoon, like around three?"

The question stunned me.

"Yeah, I guess so. Why?"

"There's a gallery in Soho that's showing an exhibit of a new local artist. I thought you might like to see it." He sounded nervous.

"With you?" I felt like an idiot as I blurted the words.

"Yeah."

Together?

"Um, yeah. OK," I said.

"Why don't we meet at my place," Devin suggested.

A date? Isn't this a violation of our contract?

"OK."

"See you later," he said.

"OK."

I hung up the phone, my hand shaking and heart pounding. What the hell just happened? Why hadn't I reminded him about the contract? Especially since *he* was the one who just broke it—Mr. You-absolutely-cannot-fall-in-love-with-me, Mr. No-socializing-otherwise-all-bets-are-off, Mr. All-business-all-the-time? Should I call him back and tell him that? Should I cancel? Should I not even go? What should I wear?

I showed up at his place around two forty-five wearing a linen pencil skirt and a white cotton shirt. Casual, yet not too datey, I thought. He wore jeans and a T-shirt. My God, he was so gorgeous, especially in jeans and a T-shirt. His face lit up when he saw me.

"You look nice."

I tried to hide a smile, but failed.

"Why do you do that?" he asked.

"Do what?"

"Force yourself not to smile when someone pays you a compliment."

"I wasn't doing that. I was just, I don't know what I was doing—do I do that a lot?"

"You've got a great smile, Andi. Don't hide it."

I did it again. He emanated an enormous, electric grin to which I couldn't help but respond with one of my own.

As we headed to Soho, he filled me in on the exhibit and the artist.

"You really know this stuff, huh," I said. He shrugged, as if to say, *It's no big deal.* "Why don't you pursue it? It's not too late, you know." I quickly added, "How old are you, anyway? If you don't mind my asking."

He cocked an eyebrow. "Thirty-eight. And nah, I already have a job. Besides, being in the art business is a lot more pressure than people realize. It's also extremely hard to get into, like music or acting."

"I'm sure with your contacts and networking abilities, you'd have no problem."

"But I like being an escort."

Something about this last statement troubled me, and a sense of hopelessness settled in.

The gallery was small and empty; thus, it didn't take long to view the exhibit. I found myself more fixated on the fact that Devin and I were there together, violating the contract, than on the paintings. Afterwards, he turned to me.

"Wanna get something to eat?"

My reflexive smile-hiding turned into a contorted look of someone who'd just sucked a lemon, peel and all.

"OK."

We walked down the street and around the corner to a restaurant just as tiny as the gallery yet almost filled to capacity.

"So what'd you think of the exhibit?" Devin asked me after we were seated.

I took in a breath, afraid of saying something stupid. "It was good."

I sounded like my students during their first peer review. Good essay. Good word choice. Good start.

"Just good?" he asked.

"I mean, I obviously don't have the eye that you have," I added.

"You don't need one to enjoy it."

"Well, I did—enjoyed it, I mean. What did you think of it?"

"I think it shows promise. The silk-screen paintings looked a little muddy to me; other than that, though..." He trailed off.

"What do you mean by 'muddy'?" I asked.

"To me, silk-screen colors should be clear, vibrant. These just looked messy. The colors were…" he tried to think of a word, "…I don't know, *muddy*. Like a kid mixing all his finger paints together, or dipping your Easter eggs into every single dye."

I laughed; I used to do both when I was a kid.

His eyes sparkled. "I like your laugh, Andi."

Before I had a chance to react, the server came to take our orders. I chose the classic spaghetti and meatballs, while Devin ordered the primavera and roasted vegetables along with a glass of wine, which he named by brand and grape. "And a ginger ale in a wine glass for the professor," he said with a wink as he gestured to me. The server smiled at me politely before whisking the menu from my hands. After she left, Devin then turned to me. "Sorry, I didn't wanna call you *lady*, and *her* just sounded rude."

I nodded. "Word choice," I said. "It makes all the difference in the world."

"I've been really conscious of that lately."

Say something witty, say something witty, say something witty…

"So, have you been to Long Island lately?" I asked.

Definitely not witty. Not even a distant cousin of witty.

Devin shook his head. "Not in a few weeks. I used to have a client in Manhasset, but she stopped calling. I think she finally met someone and started dating him. The only other occasion I have is to see family, and I'm not much of a family guy."

"They know what you do for a living?"

He nodded and raised his eyebrows. "Oh yeah."

"And they disapprove," I said more as a statement than a question.

"Yeah." The server returned with our drinks, and he practically gulped half of his upon his answer. Touchy subject, I'd gathered.

"Tell me about your family, and growing up on the Island. Did you like it? You came back, obviously, so you must have."

I sipped my ginger ale and coughed once. "Yeah, I liked it, I guess. I didn't have anything else to compare it to until I left. I've always loved being near the ocean—not *on* it, mind you, but near it. On it makes me a little seasick."

"What about *in* it?"

"Depends on how strong the undertow is. I almost got carried away by it when I was a kid. Thankfully, my older brother was close enough to pull me to safety."

"You really look up to your brothers, don't you."

I nodded. "They've always looked out for me. Even before my father died. They used to read to me and let me tag along with them and their girlfriends to Jones Beach, and they even used to let me help them record. We had a studio in our basement, and I used to come down and just listen to them for hours. I used to do things like adjust the mic stands if I could reach them, or I used to press the Record, Stop, and Play buttons on the tape machine, that sort of thing."

"How come you never took up an instrument yourself?"

Because I was no good at it, I heard a voice say. "I tried to play the drums when I was a kid. And they both tried to teach me guitar, of course. But I didn't have the patience to learn. And they had all the talent. Not that I'm tone deaf or anything like that. I probably listen to music the way you look at a piece of art. I hear more than just the song; I hear all the little nuances of the composition."

"Well phrased," he said.

"I suppose I look at writing the same way. Writing was always my thing, from day one. And teaching, I guess. My brothers are lousy teachers," I joked.

"You're a very good teacher," he said, his tone serious.

"So are you."

"What do you write?"

"Mostly memoirs, personal essays. The kinds of things I'm having you read and write."

"I'd love to read it some day."

"*My* stuff?" I asked, taken back by the question, for some reason.

"Sure, why not?"

"It's been a while since I showed it to anyone," I said. *You mean, since you showed it to a guy,* I thought. *A guy you like...*

"I'll bet it's good."

"Maybe," I said. "Maybe you'll think it's muddy."

He laughed.

This was nice. Natural.

Our orders arrived.

"So tell me something about *your* family and *your* experience of the Island," I said as I used my spoon to twirl my spaghetti around my fork. "Do you have any brothers and sisters?"

"Two sisters," he said before biting into a forkful of pasta. "Mmmm," he said while chewing, "this is good." He then finished chewing and continued, "I'm the middle child. They both still live on the Island. One's a soccer mom and the other is an administrative assistant for some company. I wouldn't call us a close family. My dad…" He trailed off. "My dad doesn't think too much of me."

I had gathered that much from his memoir.

"I'm sorry to hear that. If it makes you feel any better, I don't think my mom thinks too much of me."

"Then let's not waste a good meal on them," he said, holding up his wine glass and waiting for me to do the same. I picked mine up and raised it to his. "Cheers," he said.

"To beautiful things," I said, looking straight at him and averting my eyes at the last nanosecond.

"Hear, hear."

We clinked glasses and drank. Devin paused before continuing, as if the moment actually moved him.

"As for life on the Island, well, I was your average kid who biked everywhere with his buddies and got suspended for smoking in the boys' room once and bought records at Record World."

"And you looked at art books and went to museums. Yep. Average kid."

"And you buried your nose in every other kind of book, I'll bet," he retorted, wearing a sly grin.

"More or less. I went through phases."

"Please tell me you didn't have Boy George posters when you were a teenager."

"Simon LeBon," I replied.

"He was cool."

"And you?"

"Charlie's Angels."

I rolled my eyes around. Of course. "No Janet Jackson or Debbie Gibson?"

"Debbie Gibson was way too young for me. Janet wasn't my kind of music."

So how did this average kid wind up sexually servicing women for a living? I wanted to ask him. At what point did he decide that this was a good career move? Had he mentioned it to his guidance counselor in high school? Did he read a brochure? Were there recruitment days? I said none of it. Instead, I continued to grill him on musical tastes and which high school he went to and why he preferred the city to the suburbs.

The time whisked by in fast motion, and at some point I stepped outside of myself and observed us, completely at ease with each other, laughing and sharing more stories about growing up on Long Island before moving on to my time in Massachusetts. As I recounted my first visit to Boston and getting lost trying to find the *Cheers* bar, my brothers visiting and insisting we make a pilgrimage to the Samuel Adams Pub (their Junior's—I sat there and drank water while they sampled beer as if at a wine tasting), my chest felt a pang for Boston and all its history and accents and asymmetrical setup. And Devin listened, so attentive, so interested, so present. It was as if we were the only two in the restaurant. As if we were dating.

When the server brought us the check, Devin refused to let me pay for my dinner.

"Don't worry about it," he said.

"But, Devin…"

"It's my treat."

"Thanks," I said, a hint of doubt in my voice as I tried to read the gesture: was this *I'm a nice guy and this was my idea so I'm paying*, or *we're on a date and I'm a gentleman so I'm paying*?

After dinner, when we exited the restaurant and stepped out onto the sidewalk, dusk setting in, he stopped and looked both ways, then turned to me.

"Wanna catch a movie or something?"

The invitation left me feeling both exhilarated and confused. What was going on here? Was he afraid to go home? Come to think of it, why wasn't he on a date with a client? He was always booked. And yet, I couldn't bring myself to confront him. If I reminded him about the contract, it meant that we'd have to stop the sessions, and I didn't want to do that. Plus, he'd have to pay me for services rendered, and frankly, I had no idea how to do the math on that. Besides, he could refuse, or insist that I pay him (which was far more costly) on the grounds that I had agreed to go with him. (I could picture us on *The People's Court*—the old one, with Judge Wapner and Rusty the Bailiff—trying to explain the contract: "Well, you see, Your Honor, we had this arrangement...")

There was also the possibility that this was not a date, just an innocent outing between friends, for lack of a better word. Or, perhaps even more frightening, it *was* a date. What if he kissed me? What if he wanted to sleep with me? Would it count as part of our arrangement? Would he find out the real reason why I wanted and needed the instruction in the first place?

I opted to keep quiet.

"It's getting kind of late. I really oughta get back to the Island. I have work to do tomorrow."

"You can always stay at my place—on the couch, I mean."

A sensation not unlike a swift kick in the stomach crossed with the deflation of a tire overtook me. I couldn't imagine anyone sleeping on Devin's couch. Sitting on it was one thing, but sleeping on it? It would protest, get a restraining order. Heck, calling it a "couch" seemed an insult.

"Thanks anyway. This was nice. I haven't hung out in the city like this in a while."

He rode the subway with me to Penn Station, and even offered to ride the LIRR with me in order to make sure I got home safely.

"I'm fine," I said. "Really, thanks."

"OK, Andi. See ya."

I waited for a kiss, a hug…*something*. I'd seen him kiss Allison the textbook rep on the cheek. But here and now, nothing. Not even a handshake.

I rode home, staring past my reflection in the blackness of the window, replaying every word and movement of the day. A very young couple sat a few rows diagonally ahead of me, in the seats that faced the opposite direction. Her head rested on his shoulder, strands of blond-streaked hair falling into her eyes, and he gingerly pushed them out and over her ear, without disturbing her sleep. He then kissed the top of her head and laid his hand on her leg before closing his own eyes, as if life were perfect in that moment for him. And it probably was. He looked a little bit like a younger version of Andrew.

NINE

Week Five of the Arrangement

THIS WAS NOT GOOD.

Ever since Thursday, I held vigil with my phone and telepathically willed it to ring; otherwise, I compulsively checked the answering machine to see if Devin had called while I was in the shower, or out getting the mail, or running an errand. Nothing.

In the meantime, I tried to keep busy. I went to Jones Beach and tried to read, or to Starbucks with my laptop and tried to write, and yet again out to lunch with my mother. We sat facing each other in the Northport Restaurant & Diner, my mother commenting about how the necklines of my tops were getting lower.

My mother had always been rather striking—she was one of those moms who would wear slacks and a full face of makeup when she went food shopping, her hair neatly coiffed and her accessories all matching. When my father died, she spent months in bed and let the gray roots grow out. Wrinkles appeared on her pained face seemingly overnight. And then, as she slowly rejoined the living and I progressed through my hellish adolescence, Mom did more than put on a happy face. She got cosmetic surgery, took up jogging, and updated her wardrobe. I, on the other hand, fought with frizzy hair, Snickers bars, and lots of pairs of leggings and hand-me-down Lee jeans. Growing up with two brothers, I'd never had much instruction on how to put an outfit together. You'd think Mom would've offered a hand. But all she gave me was criticism. Looking back, it was as if she and I were in competition for good fashion sense and appeal, and she would not be outdone.

Today, Mom was back to her put-together persona. Her hair now a lustrous silver bob and her makeup straight out of Lancome's exclusive line, she looked ten years younger and like she ran a corporation in the pantsuit she donned, the jacket resting comfortably on her bare shoulders and silk camisole. The air-conditioning was too high, she complained.

"So, what have you been up to?" she asked after we ordered.

"Just your typical summer stuff," I said, avoiding eye contact. "You know, summer reading, working on my essays, hanging out with friends."

"Anyone I know?"

"Oh, just my friends Maggie and Jayce," I said as the sane and insane parts of my brain held a quick debate on whether I should mention Devin. Guess who lost. "And I've been going into the city once a week to take a class. It's sort of a self-help class."

She looked at me, her eyes burning with suspicion.

"What kind of self-help?"

Aw, crap. I regretted this instantly.

"Oh, you know, the usual."

"No, I don't know. What kind of help do you need? I mean, I know you had a rough time after Andrew cheated on you…"

Leave it to my mother to use those words…

"…but you're fine now. You're working and paying your bills and going out."

"Mom, it's—I'm—I wanna better myself. What's wrong with that?"

"I just think you're wasting your money, that's all. You're fine."

Apparently I'd gotten good at faking it with everyone, including my mother. Rather than turn my snowball lie into an avalanche, I refrained from saying anything about bartering my services and instead signaled the waitress to order a big cookie.

"Should you be eating that?" she asked when the waitress returned seconds later.

As I stared her down, mentally ordering laser beams to shoot out from my eyeballs, I chomped into my cookie and said nothing. Hell yes.

———

The following Tuesday, Devin called and asked if we could move our meeting time to around seven thirty.

"What, no client tonight?" I asked.

"I canceled."

"Why?"

"I thought I'd show you the finer pleasures of a bathtub date."

"You're kidding me."

"Dead serious."

I pulled the phone away from my ear for a second and dropped my mouth open.

"And you can't do this at two in the afternoon?" I asked.

"It's not the same when it's so bright outside. You need the proper atmosphere—candles and that sort of thing."

I agreed to meet him, and then called Maggie immediately afterwards to tell her.

"Can you believe he actually canceled a client for this? Do you know how much money he loses when he does that?"

"Obviously he wants to be with you instead," she said. My heart fluttered, although I shrugged off the notion.

"I'll bet his partner's going to be pissed," I said.

"He probably got someone else to fill in for him. Face it: this is no ordinary escort."

"You know, I just thought of something: should I bring a swimsuit?"

"Why would you do that?"

"Well, it's either that or get naked."

"Isn't that the whole point?"

"I guess so. What have I gotten myself into, Mags?" I asked her that at least once a week since I'd started meeting Devin.

"Bring a change of underwear, just in case."

"In case what?"

"Well gosh, if you have to ask!" Maggie said with a laugh. My face burned in the privacy of my apartment, and I abruptly ended the call.

I showed up wearing jeans, a light blue tank top, and flip-flops, but brought no wardrobe changes. My hair had grown out quite a bit, almost long enough for a ponytail. It fell in waves, and I kept it out of my face with a headband. Devin looked comfortable in his usual jeans and a faded U2 Elevation concert tour T-shirt. He was barefoot and sporting a salon-induced tan, his brown hair perfectly coiffed, as always, with a few orangey-blond streaks in his bangs.

For my portion of the session, I introduced the concepts of argument and classical rhetoric, and we discussed *Phaedrus*, Plato's slam against the sophists and philosophical foray into provisional versus absolute truth, which confounded Devin.

I explained, "The sophists were the talk show hosts, televangelists, and motivational speakers of their time. The Stephen Colberts. Orators for hire—have quill, will travel. And they were regarded as rock stars with their grandiloquent ability to move the masses and make them swoon."

"Sounds like a good gig."

"Plato didn't think so. He's saying that sophistry is nothing more than 'cookery,' a bunch of bells and whistles, and that rhetoric is not so much a pursuit of truth as much as a means of persuasion."

"So, when you called me 'a modern-day sophist,' you weren't paying me a compliment?"

I started to open my mouth but then stopped short. Good fucking memory.

"But here's the cool thing," I said, ignoring his comment. "If you really study the text, Plato is *teaching*, and he uses metaphor and tropes used in rhetoric to do so."

"So?"

"*So?* Do you realize that this is the stuff that I'm still teaching to this day? Metaphor? Rhetoric as a means of communication and persuasion? He paved the way for guys like Aristotle who systematized the whole thing, modes of discourse and all."

"And truth?" he asked.

"What about truth?"

"Is rhetoric a means to truth or not?"

"Plato didn't think so. He thought sophistic rhetoric actually got in the way of the search for absolute truth, which sort of contradicts what I teach today. I say language is a way to make meaning, to express truth in many forms. Plato sought to use rhetoric analytically and dialectically. Read the text again and you'll see it—look at the dialectic between Socrates and Phaedrus."

He frowned. You'd think I'd offered him a second helping of liver. "I'll pass," he said in feigned politeness.

"It's an acquired taste," I replied.

When our writing session was finished (first I had him describe the Warhol painting without using any of the words typically found in an art review; then I had him write an impromptu speech—he even created a metaphor inspired by the Platonic "cookery," which impressed me further), Devin left the living room to prepare the bath, while once again I circled the loft to admire his art collection. He'd added a new piece—a small, square-shaped oil on canvas that featured various shades of hot red layers broken up by a yellow stripe running across the top, looking like torn paper. Very abstract.

"Ready," he called.

I entered the bathroom. The room glowed with votives strategically placed around the massive jet-stream tub brimming with suds, and smelled of lavender and vanilla. Thick, plush towels were folded spa style and relaxed at the tub's edge. Soft, jazzy music reverberated off the walls, and I couldn't even find the speakers. I sucked in my breath.

"Wow," I said, my voice barely audible.

"You like?"

I nodded. "Heaven."

"Well, get in."

I looked at him hesitantly.

"Am I supposed to get naked?"

"It would kill the mood to wear your clothes, don't you think?"

"Do I have other options?"

"Did you bring a swimsuit?"

My face flushed. "No."

"Then no, you have no other options. If you were so concerned, why didn't you bring a swimsuit? It's not like you didn't know what was coming."

"You didn't tell me to."

"That's because a swimsuit defeats the purpose."

"Well geez, this tub is about the size of a pool."

He laughed and looked at it with approval, as if he'd built it himself. "So, are you getting in, or are you waiting for an engraved invitation?"

I looked at the tub, the bubbles making fizzy, muffled, snap-crackle-pop noises, and contemplated my decision. *Why not?*

"OK. Don't look," I said. He left the room. I stripped naked, leaving my clothes in a small heap at the base of the tub and stepped in, careful not to let the suds or any water spill over. The water was warm and smooth like velvet; I gathered as much foam as I could to cover myself, and then leaned back against the terrycloth pillow, closing my eyes.

"OK," I called. "I'm in."

Devin came back with two Mikasa flutes—ginger ale for me and champagne for him (he had started keeping ginger ale in his fridge just for me). He looked at me, delighted. I blushed in the shadow cast by the candlelight.

"How's the water?" His voice, mellow and sonorous, matched the mood.

"Divine," I replied, giving in with every passing second. He knelt beside me at the edge of the tub before I closed my eyes again. I could almost feel a magnetic aura around him, pulling us together.

"So, whaddya want? Want me to sponge your back, shampoo your hair, rub your feet…what?"

"You really do this with your clients?"

"If that's what they ask for, yes."

"What else do they ask for?"

"To bathe other body parts."

While my imagination filled in which parts, I opened my eyes and sat up slightly, my softened muscles contracting again. Devin dropped his hand into the water and swished it back and forth.

"Aw, Andi, you were beginning to let go—I could see it on your face. Now you're all tense again. How come?"

"In my house, we didn't talk about 'body parts.' GTO parts, yes. Guitar parts, absolutely. Not body parts."

He rolled his eyes, then muttered, "Good God, it's a wonder you were even conceived. Where were your parents when Vatican II came out?"

Where was my mother? I thought. As I recalled dinnertime conversations, it seemed that my father and brothers dominated my memories, as well as the conversations. I couldn't remember my mother ever interjecting other than to ask who wanted seconds or to clear the table. Come to think of it, I couldn't remember ever getting a word in edgewise. Why? It's not like my brothers ignored me completely. Rather, they often invited me to come with them to Howard Johnson's for an ice cream soda with their friends, or let me sit and watch when they rehearsed. Their interests interested me. It just didn't seem reciprocal.

"I don't know," was the only answer I could muster.

"It's just a body, after all," he said.

"A body is one thing. Body parts are completely different, though. Just saying the words 'body parts' makes you wanna take a shower. At least in my family it does."

"That's ridiculous. Why is a *body* sterile and scientific, or a work of art, but *body parts* are shameful and taboo? It makes no sense. How are body parts any less natural or aesthetic than the whole body?"

"A body is more than the sum of its gross parts?"

"I'm not kiddin'."

"Neither am I, Dev." My on-the-spot creation and use of a nickname for him momentarily surprised me, but I continued. "There are some body parts that I wouldn't exactly wanna photograph and frame. Take the nose, for example. An ugly protrusion with holes and hair in it. Ew.

Did you ever meet anyone who said, 'Whoa, check out the nose on that girl!' Then there's…"

Ignoring my rambling, Devin stood up, stripped down to his boxers, and stepped into the tub, sitting across from me. I sat up as straight as I could without revealing my bare breasts, trying to inch my way back.

"Relax," he said. "There's plenty of room for both of us, and I'm not going to look at or touch any part of you that you don't want me to see or touch. But for the record, I've seen and touched enough naked bodies to know—"

"—to know that all bodies are beautiful. Yeah, you used that line on me before."

"It's not a line," he said, irked. "And I was gonna say, to know how to make a woman forget her self-consciousness."

He had his work cut out for him tonight. And he read my mind at that instant.

"Tell you what. We'll just talk—about anything you want. Music, the weather…you see the game last night?"

We started talking about the Yankees game, and next thing I knew, it was as if we were sitting across from each other at Junior's rather than in a candlelit bathtub. It occurred to me then that my initial resistance had little to do with self-consciousness and more to do with the fact that I actually *wanted* him to see and touch my bare body, to find it desirable. Pretty soon I moved closer to him, first running my foot along his calf, then turning around so that he was behind me, caressing a lavender-scented puffy sponge along my neck and down my back while we talked quietly. And, sure enough, I forgot all about my self-consciousness and my naked body and leaned into the protection of his firm, sturdy arms. That night, I understood the secret of why his clients kept coming back for more. Indeed, he knew how to make each one feel sexy, uninhibited, beautiful, and like each one was the only woman in the world.

But how did *he* feel? I wondered. Was he aroused? Fighting to keep from doing more than just sponging my back? Or was I just another client? Had he successfully learned to emotionally and physically detach himself from the women he serviced? Was that even possible? After all, he was a man. Unless he was gay…was that it?

As the votives started to go out and the suds broke up, he stood up and reached for the full-length towel waiting for me. I tried to look for signs of an erection, but he was too quick for me.

"Here." He closed his eyes and held the towel out in front of him and open for me, still standing there, dripping. "Say when."

His gesture struck me; he'd just spent the last hour— or more—with my naked body, and yet he still respected my privacy without judgment. I stood up and moved into the butter-soft towel as he practically hugged me with it before I stepped out.

"My God, this feels good. Did you use the whole bottle of fabric softener?"

"That's cute. Can I open my eyes now?"

"Oh yeah, sorry. Thanks."

"You're welcome." He quickly stepped out of the tub and grabbed a towel for himself. "So? What'd you think?"

"I think we should start doing *this* once a week from now on."

He grinned. "You did great. You relaxed and got comfortable with me. I'm proud of you."

I glowed. Then I looked at him, perplexed.

"Why'd you get into the tub with me? You said you don't usually do that."

"The situation warranted it—you needed the presence of a man's body, and to see that there's nothing sinful about it."

"If that's the case, then why didn't you get completely naked?"

"I didn't want to overwhelm you. I mean…" He blushed and looked away, laughing nervously. It was nice to see I wasn't the only one who got flustered.

"You're that good, huh?" I said, more friendly than flirtatious.

He didn't answer me—didn't need to. I could feel a connection between us at that moment, and liked it.

I then wondered why I'd never spent an evening like this with Andrew. In fact, I don't think I'd ever had such an intimate encounter with anyone. Not that Andrew didn't want to do such sexy, romantic things with me. He would take me out for candlelit dinners or serenade me with a folk song that he wrote just for me, but I'd avoided many of his more personal advances, and suddenly I couldn't for the life of me figure out why. Why had I never *trusted* him? I was engaged to him, after all. How could I be more trusting of a man I'd never even kissed, a man I barely knew, than of my fiancé?

Devin peered at his watch in the dimness of the room, then moved in close to me, pulling my towel tighter, encasing me in its safety like a cocoon.

"I think we're done for the day," he said, standing before me, looking into my eyes and transfixing me.

I gave him a ditzy nod. "OK." I gazed some more before asking, "What time is it?"

"A little after ten."

"Mmmmmmm."

Kiss me.

"It's getting late," he said.

"Yeah."

KISS ME!!!

"Wanna stay over?"

"OK."

Please?

He left the room and came back with a folded black T-shirt. "Here," he said, and tossed it to me; being that I was practically straight-jacketed in the towel, it carelessly bounced off my bound arm and fell to the floor without making a sound. Then he said, "I'll take the couch."

The words hit me in the head, jarring me back to consciousness. The *couch?*

"You sure?" I asked, trying to hide both my disappointment and confusion. Had he not just asked me to spend the night with him? Were we twelve? Was he going to make popcorn so we could stay up all night and watch Duran Duran videos?

"It's no problem."

I silently finished drying off and put on the T-shirt while he changed the linens on his bed. Then I went to the bed and crept under the covers. Like the towels, the sheets were magnificently soft.

"Devin?"

"Yeah?"

"Why did you ask me to stay over?"

"You were too blissed out to take the train home at this time of night. I didn't want anything to happen to you."

"Oh." I didn't know whether to appreciate his thoughtfulness or be annoyed at his misleading behavior.

"G'night, Andi. Sleep well."

"Thanks. You too." Before he could leave, I called out to him again.

"Hey, Dev?"

"Yeah?"

"Thank you for this. For canceling your client tonight, I mean. That must have cost you some money."

His face softened into an expression of satisfaction. "G'night," he said again.

He turned out the light, and I inhaled the scent of him on the sheets and the T-shirt until I had no choice but to succumb to slumber.

TEN

I AWOKE THE NEXT morning to the shrill siren of a fire
engine racing down the block, and had a momentary
lapse of memory. One whiff of the sheets brought me
back, however, and I sat up in bed, looking around the
room. The walls were painted sage green and looked
different in sunlight as opposed to the shadowy dimness
of the previous night. Brighter. Classy. A lithograph of
an etched landscape hung on the wall opposite the bed,
and I had a sudden desire to jump through it and enter
its world, just as Julie Andrews and Dick Van Dyke and
the kids had done in *Mary Poppins.*

In contrast to the commotion of the city, even at—what
time was it, anyway?—the apartment was eerily still and
silent. I turned and looked at the clock on the nightstand
to my right. 9:14.

Where was Devin?

The bedroom was partitioned off from the rest of the
loft. I leaned as far over the edge of the bed as I could to
see if he was in the living room, when I lost my balance
and fell off, banging my elbow.

Shit!

I pulled myself up quickly, expecting Devin to respond

to the thud, race in, and find me tangled in bedsheets on the floor. But the place resumed its idleness following my noisy tumble. Still wearing his T-shirt, I tentatively wandered out like a skittish cat, calling out once, "Devin?" and hearing only the scant echo of his name. I felt as if I had infiltrated an art gallery before its opening, as if I were somewhere I shouldn't be.

The bathroom door was open, the snuffed-out votives still in their places. The sofa showed no evidence of having been slept on. No rumpled sheets or pillows with cranium-shaped indentations in them. I checked all counters and tabletops for a note. Nothing.

He's not here.

I sat on the sofa for about ten minutes, completely stymied, staring at the door, practically willing him to enter.

Why would he just leave me here? Was he coming back?

My mind searched for an explanation: Maybe he had an early morning client. Maybe his leaving me to fend for myself was part of his instruction. Maybe he was off teaching some other repressed yutz to be a better lover; maybe he'd branched off in a side business, thanks to me. Maybe he was out buying new votive candles. Or maybe he was buying food so he could cook me breakfast when he got back. That would be nice.

Another five minutes of deadened silence passed. The door remained closed, locked. What was I supposed to do? Wait for him? For how much longer?

I stood up.

"Screw this."

I went to the bathroom. There were new towels just as

neatly folded as the night before. Travel-sized soaps and deodorant, shampoo bottles with top-of-the-line brand names, and a new toothbrush sat on the sink counter next to the towels. But no note. In the bedroom, my clothes were folded perfectly on the chair beside the bed, which meant that he'd been in the room at some point while I was asleep, because I'd left them in a heap on the bathroom floor the night before. And still no note.

I changed and contemplated whether to take his T-shirt with me. I should wash it, I thought. But would I give it back?

I crumpled the shirt into a ball and tried to shove it into my purse. It bulged and burst out the top. Just as I headed for the door, it opened and Devin walked in, juggling two tall coffee cups and a paper bag.

"Hey!" he said, sounding surprised to see me. As he looked me up and down, hyperawareness of my matted and mussed hair and my blotchy face kicked in.

"You're leaving?" he asked. "I got bagels for us."

"Did you have a layover in Cleveland or something?"

He laughed. "There's a great place six blocks up with a line out the door. It's worth the wait, though, you'll see." He plopped the bag on the kitchen island, placing the cups more slowly. "I got you a chai latte and a half-dozen bagels—plain, pumpernickel, multigrain, an everything for me…"

So, this was breakfast with Devin.

My voice was MIA.

"You sleep OK?" he asked.

"Yeah, it was fine."

"Good."

"How 'bout you?" I asked.

"Fine." He smiled and his eyes sparkled. He took two blue ceramic plates from a shelf above the sink and put them on the island, then held the bag open for me. "So? Take your pick."

"Um, I gotta go."

His smile vanished and the sparkles in his eyes extinguished. "How come? There's no rush. I don't have to work until tonight."

"I've got an orientation planning meeting that I'm gonna be late for if I don't get a move-on," I lied. "I still gotta shower and change."

"You can shower here, ya know. I left everything out for you."

"Yeah, I saw that. Thanks, but I still need to change and get my briefcase."

"You don't even have time to sit and eat?"

I shook my head.

Clearly disappointed, he looked down at the empty plate designated for me.

"I guess I shouldn't have let you sleep late. Well, at least take a bagel with you for the road."

"Thanks," I said, taking a plain bagel and half of the pile of napkins he'd grabbed from the store.

"Cream cheese? Butter?"

"Plain is fine."

He then pushed one of the cups toward me. "Don't forget your chai."

"Thanks."

We stood on opposite sides of the island, looking at each other as if playing a game of "chicken."

"Well," I started (I knew I'd lose), "thanks again for last night, and for letting me stay over."

"You're welcome." He then noticed the T-shirt ball spilling out of my purse.

"Oh, did you want your shirt back? I was gonna wash it for you."

"No need."

Disappointed, I pulled the ball out as it uncrumpled, and quickly scanned for a place to put it. Devin extended his hand. "I got it," he said.

Reluctantly, I let go of it.

"Well," I said, "I'm late."

"OK. Well, see ya."

"Yeah, OK."

We walked to the door, and he opened and held it for me. Just as I was about to leave, bagel and chai in tow, he leaned in and pecked me on the cheek; the gesture startled me so much I nearly jerked back to dodge it.

"See ya," he said again.

I practically ran to the subway until I stopped.

"Wait a minute...what am I doing?" I said out loud—I'd managed to convince *myself* that I really had a meeting to go to, when I actually had nothing planned for the day.

On the platform, caught in a wild pack of commuters rushing the open train doors and another wild pack trying to get off the train, my bagel was knocked out of my hand and rolled carelessly onto the tracks, no doubt to be consumed by the rodents below. By the time the train reached Penn Station, I was completely dejected. Before boarding the LIRR, I threw out the cup of chai latte; it was still more than half-full.

ELEVEN

"I DON'T GET IT," Maggie said as she dumped her third packet of Sweet'N Low into her iced coffee. "Why'd you leave?"

Maggie and I sat in a booth at the Empress Diner off Wantagh Parkway. I'd called her as the train left Penn Station and had asked her to meet me there for lunch. I needed a friend.

"I don't know. I just had to get out of there. I couldn't take it anymore."

"Couldn't take what?"

"The disappointment. First he reels me in with this super-sexy bathtub date, then he invites me to spend the night but sleeps on the sofa. Then, I wake up and he's not even in the apartment. And then he comes back with a bag of *bagels*—not *breakfast*, mind you, but take-out food. Hell, I can walk down the street and get one myself."

"What were you expecting, a buffet? Really, Andi, I think you're being too hard on him. How do you know he wasn't gonna fix it up nice and serve it to you in bed?"

She had a point. I didn't know.

"Besides, this was all part of the instruction, wasn't it? It wasn't supposed to be an actual date. And he didn't have to invite you to stay. He could've just let you go wander in the street last night, on your little endorphin high. If you ask me, I'd say he gave you quite a bit of consideration."

She had a point there, too.

"Then why does he keep stopping short?" I asked. "I mean, if he goes to such great lengths to spend time with me or take care of me, then why doesn't he go all the way?"

It was a good question, I thought. He didn't go all the way with his clients, either. Why?

"Why don't *you*?" she asked. "You've had just as many opportunities to kiss him, haven't you?"

Damn, she was getting base hits all over the place.

"I can't," I said.

"Why not?"

"I don't know." That was the truth. Something stopped me every time. Maybe it was a fear of rejection. Maybe it was the damn contract. Whatever it was, it was starting to annoy me.

"Look, if you're this upset about it, then maybe you ought to tell him. Or stop the whole arrangement."

If I told him that I had wanted, hoped for more the night before, then I'd have to admit that I had feelings for him, and I had no intention of going there. For one thing, it would be yet another violation of our contract. For another, I feared he'd tell me that I was a fool for getting sucked into an illusion. Lord knows that even after all this time, I still felt the sting of Andrew's rejection and the humiliation of falsely hoping that I (or he) was worth waiting for.

No, my only option was to fake it, play it cool, pretend like I wanted and needed nothing more, not even the bagel, to walk out feeling satisfied. Little did I know that when it came to Devin, I fooled no one, least of all him.

———————

Later that afternoon, he called me.

"Just wanted to make sure you got to your meeting on time," he said.

"Oh, yeah. It was fine." I felt guilty about prolonging the lie. "I really am sorry about rushing out the way I did this morning."

"No problem."

I paused for a beat. "So hey, you wanna come out here tonight to watch the game or a DVD or something?"

Where did that come from?

Devin, without missing a beat, responded, "Can't. Got a client tonight, remember? How 'bout tomorrow afternoon? We can catch a matinee. Is the Shore Theatre in Huntington Village still around?"

"I think so."

"Great, then let's do that. Geez, I haven't been there in ages."

"Me neither," I said.

I waited for him to say, "It's a date." But instead, he said, "You know, I tried to read that Plato stuff again after you left."

A goofy grin escaped from me at that moment; you'd think he said, *You know, I've been thinking about you all day.*

"And?"

"And I still don't get it."

"Then read it again."

"Can't I just get the Cliff Notes?"

I laughed. "Man, are you out of touch. These days the students use 'Spark Notes,' and they're all online. And I don't think they have 'em for *Phaedrus*."

"Well, they should."

We chatted for a few more minutes about getting through most of Shakespeare and Homer in high school thanks to Cliff Notes, and concluded with my agreeing to pick him up at the Hicksville station the next day.

After we got off the phone, I went to my computer, opened up Google, and typed in "sparknotes" followed by a search of "Phaedrus." It produced ten hits. Surprised, I perused them and considered printing them out for Devin. Nah, I thought. Let him figure it out by himself.

TWELVE

I WAITED FOR DEVIN on the platform at the Hicksville station, and together we got into my blue Corolla and drove to downtown Huntington, which had become as crowded as any Manhattan street, while bars, pizza places, Greek restaurants, coffee shops, law offices, specialty stores, and apparel boutiques lined Main and Wall Streets and New York Avenue. The Shore Theatre, on the corner of Wall Street at the center of town, was the gathering place for my friends and me throughout our teens on Friday and Saturday nights. Once home to four dingy theaters, the Shore had done an extreme makeover after a fire destroyed part of it. The renovations included new theaters, stadium seating, state-of-the-art sound systems, and a new name, the Shore Multiplex, now owned by some cinema corporation.

We got two matinee tickets to see *The Bourne Supremacy* and were two of five people in the theater on a Thursday afternoon in early August. Despite my objections, Devin insisted on paying for the tickets. "To thank you for driving," he said. We sat in two aisle seats towards the back. A middle-aged man sat alone about five rows up from us, in the middle of the row, and a woman and man in business attire sat together in the last row, under the projector.

"Do you think they're playing hooky from work and are here to fuck each other?" Devin whispered to me while a computer-animated hot dog on screen asked the audience to please turn off their cell phones.

"Do you think they're actually married to other people?" I whispered back.

"Do you think they're wondering the same thing about us?"

"Not based on where we're sitting, no."

He smiled. Geez, even in the darkness of the theater, his eyes sparkled.

Devin was a talker during movies, I found out. And not just about what was happening on the screen, but about normal life, too. For example, when Matt Damon crept down the corridor of a building, Devin leaned over and proceeded to tell me that it looked like a building in the city that one of his clients owned and made him play hide-and-seek with her in it one night. Under other circumstances, I'd tell him to shut up, or shove Twizzlers into his mouth; if it had been a first date, I'd have vowed not to have a second. But while he rambled on, I just sat there and listened, thinking to myself, *Please put your hand on my knee, please put your hand on my knee, please put your hand on my knee...*

I shivered and crossed my arms tightly; the theater air-conditioner must have been set to "tundra."

"Are you cold?" he asked. He wasn't even whispering anymore.

"I can't feel my toes."

He maneuvered himself in his seat to face me and awkwardly leaned over, put his arms around me—for a split second I thought we were going to make out—and moved his hands up and down rapidly on my own arms in an attempt to warm me. Not only was he blocking my view of the screen, but my body temperature shot from minus two to three hundred and sixty degrees in a matter of seconds as a result of his mere hands on my flesh.

I squirmed. "Dev, I can't see."

He stopped and leaned back in his own seat. "Sorry," he said. From the corner of my eye, I watched him stare blankly at the screen; it seemed as if he were having his own mental conversations of self-berating not unlike my own.

"I mean, thanks," I said. He nodded quietly. Was he actually embarrassed?

When the movie ended and the lights came on, I stood up and stretched, looking around. The couple in the back was gone, and I wondered when they'd left. The man in front stood up and walked out. Devin stayed in his seat.

"You like to stay for the credits, too?" I asked.

"These people worked hard to get their names on the screen. We owe them that."

"My brother Joey's song got in a movie once."

Devin's eyes widened. "Really? What movie?"

"It was an indie film. Kind of a *Sopranos* meets *When Harry Met Sally*. This man and woman from warring families become friends, yada yada yada. Joey's song was used while the mob father beat the shit out of the guy friend. Ironically, the song is called 'Peace in the Valley.' It's a jazz instrumental."

"That's really cool."

After the credits finished rolling, we came out of the theater and adjusted our eyes to the sunlight while I let the heat warm me up again. I put my sunglasses on and looked around.

"God, I haven't been here in ages," I said of the entire downtown. "Well over ten years. Fifteen, at least."

"Me too," he said. He wore two-hundred-dollar Ray Bans. "Wanna walk around a little bit? See what's changed?"

We walked all over the village, pointing to the bars and dance clubs we had used fake IDs to get into, the boarded-up dives where my brothers used to play, and the location that once housed the shoe store my mother used to take us to buy nerdy Buster Browns. As we strolled up a side street to the public parking lot, neither of us having spoken in a few minutes, Devin broke the silence.

"This is nice."

What the hell did that mean? Did he mean, *This is nice spending time with you, because it's you and I really like you as more than a friend*; or did he mean, *This is nice because it's a beautiful day and I'm a fucking escort who makes his own hours and lots of money*; or did he mean, *This is nice because you're my friend and friends do things like this together on a summer day?*

This time I decided to ask him. "Nice in what way?"

He seemed thrown by the question. "Just…nice. You're fun to hang out with."

My heart sank. I think I would've preferred the fucking escort answer.

"Thanks," I said.

"Wanna get an early dinner?" he asked.

"Sure. We'll go to Francesco's on Route 110 for some pizza. I haven't been there in ages, either."

I drove us there, where we shared half of a pepperoni pie and an order of garlic knots as well as more stories about growing up during the eighties and where we used to hang out (the Walt Whitman Mall for me; the Sunken Meadow boardwalk for him; that, or any one of the diners in or around Massapequa). Then Devin started asking me all kinds of questions about Massachusetts—comparisons, mostly. What's the seafood like? How do the beaches compare? Which city did I like better, Boston or Manhattan? Do they really say *paaahhk the caaaahh?* And so on. And as we talked, I steadily grew homesick for the flavorless bagels, the abominable pizza, and the comforting warmth of clam chowder. I found myself longing to hang out with my friends to watch baseball games or play tennis, and aching to feel and smell the sea breeze waft through my open windows as the sun went down. I missed things moving slower, even if only slightly.

"You OK?" he asked.

"Yeah," I said, my voice sounding wistful.

"You're a million miles away."

I shook my head slowly. "Just over the Braga Bridge."

We checked the LIRR schedule, and I drove him to the Huntington train station rather than all the way back to Hicksville. Facing the onslaught of evening rush hour commuters was not unlike attempting to drive down a one-way street as a herd of bulls came charging towards us. Rather than park and walk with him to the platform, I pulled over near the cabs and kept the car running.

"Well thanks, Andi."

"Yeah, it was nice," I said, kicking myself for using the "nice" word.

"I had a great time, really."

"Me too."

We both sat there for a minute, like a first date, neither of us knowing what to do and both of us refusing to make the next move. The air-conditioner whirred ostentatiously.

Just like the previous morning, he leaned in and pecked me on the cheek before I even had a chance to move or respond or kiss back.

"See ya next week," he said, and got out of the car, dodging and weaving through the crowd of oncoming commuters.

I drove back to East Meadow in silence, even oblivious to the air-conditioner. Devin was probably zooming towards Penn Station, asleep, while I inched along Jericho Turnpike, alert and preoccupied. It really had been a nice day.

THIRTEEN

August

Week Six of the Arrangement

B Y THE SIXTH WEEK, our tutorials and homework assignments had become more risqué, more challenging, and more rhetorical. While Devin had me sucking on phallic-shaped ice pops, I had him reading and writing commentaries about a recent prostitution bust in which the arresting officer allegedly raped the prostitute after she allegedly refused to give him a "freebie" in exchange for being let go with no charges. While he learned logical fallacies, I learned stretching exercises to improve my body's flexibility during various sexual positions. While I assigned him to read Aristotle's *Rhetoric*, he assigned me to watch *The Couple's Guide to Better Sex*, an instructional video that could have been more aptly titled *Jerking Off with the Joneses*.

Devin asked me to explain the modes of discourse to him, and I gave him a breakdown of the rhetorical strategies housed under the categories of exposition, narration, description, and argument. Moreover, I described and showed him how to access them as methods of organizing and arranging language to further rhetorical purpose.

"Why do you hate them so much?"

"I don't hate what they *are*; I hate the way they're *taught*." I then went into a diatribe about the teaching of the modes as separate, disconnected, linear formulas of writing that push students to usurp authentic purpose and instead focus on a finished, precise product that conforms to the modal criteria yet ultimately is stripped of original thought.

"In other words, they're taught not as the means *to* an end, but as the means *and* the end," said Devin.

"You got it, baby," I said, my adrenaline rising. "Current traditionalism in its most puritanical form." I then summarized Robert Connors's article "The Rise and Fall of the Modes of Discourse" and gave him a crash course in the history of composition studies in the American university. He listened to my lecture with a sort of twisted delight and admiration.

"You're an academic snob—you know that, don't you? How do you know you're not a fundamentalist in your own way?"

"A good writing instructor incorporates all theory and blends a number of practices. I teach the modes—my whole course doesn't revolve around them, but I maintain their necessity as well as the classical canons devised by Aristotle. I teach writing according to their specific social contexts and the genres that fall into the scope of those contexts based on rhetorical purpose and audience. My students engage in meta-cognition by reflecting on their own writing processes. But ultimately, I believe in expressivism and process method: using language to make meaning and understand the self in relation to others.

And it's not a neat package. It doesn't all work well all the time. But it works for me."

"Still, you're a snob."

"And my rhetorical theory professor loves me for it."

———

Devin also finished his memoir:

Found and Lost

When I was eleven years old, my fifth grade class took a field trip to the Museum of Modern Art in New York City to see a Picasso exhibit. I would've preferred a trip to Shea Stadium during batting practice or Jones Beach for surfing lessons; looking at paintings, however, was not my idea of a good time. Prior to the day of the visit, we'd spent a week in class learning about Picasso, but all I remember getting out of it was that he was some weird Spanish guy who was supposed to be a genius.

Being a kid from the south shore of Long Island, Manhattan didn't impress me the way it might someone from somewhere else in the country, somewhere more idyllic and less crowded. It was always there, after all. In fact, on a very clear day, one could faintly see the very tops of the twin towers from a certain point on the Northern State Parkway. (Of course, you had to be looking for them.)

Although this was my first time going to the MOMA, I had no expectations of being impressed, but rather bored. Almost immediately, those expectations diffused when I entered. The place was a castle of marble—gigantic wall after gigantic wall of paintings, sculptures, drawings, and tapestries awaited my inspection, and I could not possibly take it all in. My preoccupation with the shiny floors (perfect for sliding on with socks, and I must say I was tempted) was replaced by the docent (a term I would soon learn on my own, but to my eleven-year-old incarnation, it stood for boring old guide) who announced that our tour of the exhibit was about to begin. He was a skinny man with white hair, and he explained each painting to us as if we were art scholars here by choice and not kids bummed because Shea Stadium had been ruled out. Many of my classmates, however, were either restless or bored and showed their appreciation by making fun of both the paintings and him, mimicking his mannerisms and voice.

By the time we reached the second room of the exhibit, my classmates had stopped listening to the docent altogether. Along the way, we passed another room that caught and held my attention. I crept away from Steven Marino, my dreaded "buddy" (in title only, assigned to us for the purpose of not getting lost on field trips), and when everyone was distracted by one of Picasso's cubist renditions, I escaped.

Time stood still in this new room. The first painting I saw spanned almost the entire wall. It seemed familiar, like a finger painting from my childhood. But when I moved closer, I could see just about every imaginable color in darting, tiny brushstrokes. It was as if my eyes had become blurry and I could neither make out shape nor image; but I could clearly see the movement of the artist, as if I knew exactly what he was thinking when he painted it. When I stepped back, the colors and brushstrokes dissolved together into the form of water lilies. I circled the room, again and again, leaning in as close as I dared to each painting. I practically walked on tiptoes, afraid I'd disturb them—they looked too alive, and I was spying.

I must have been a curious sight: an eleven-year-old boy dressed in Levi's jeans, a Rolling Stones glitter T-shirt, and Adidas sneakers, so fascinated with these pictures on the wall. I didn't care. I was lost in the flurry of brushstrokes, thousands of them, all in one room. Furious and gentle, red and green, all tumbling over each other. All in one room.

The painting of a ballerina, seemingly tucked away in a corner, was the most breathtaking of all. She looked as if she would leap right out of the frame and dance just for me. She was fleeting, delicate, and sensual.

So, this was art. Picasso wasn't just a weird Spanish guy anymore, and these weren't just paintings—they were shapes, forms, and colors. Like the twin towers, you just had to know where to look. They took me to a place way beyond my childhood experience of papier-mâché and poster paints, to a world as much removed from time as I was from my classmates, until a mother chaperoning our trip found me (Steven must have squealed). She dragged me back to the bunch of schoolkids still staring at frame after frame of Picasso. I don't know if my teacher was angry at me for breaking away from the group or because I was unremorseful for my escape. I didn't even hear her scolding; instead, I saw her lips move in tiny, darting brushstrokes of red hues. Meanwhile, the docent droned at the children, the children dully eyed the Picassos, the chaperones watched me, and I saw nothing and everything: nothing that looked real, and everything in a world of brushstrokes. I wanted to make these kinds of paintings.

That night, still elated from my discovery, I announced to my parents that I was going to be an artist. I was sure of it.

My father grunted, while my mother looked up from the book she was staring at long enough to say, "That's nice."

I tried again. "Dad," I said persistently, "I'm going to be an artist—a painter."

"The only thing men paint is houses."

"But…"

"If you're so set on being an artist, then the first thing you oughta paint is a pair of fairy wings for yourself."

It was final. I said nothing and turned away.

My heart broke that day. I found and lost passion in a manner as quick and fleeting as those brushstrokes. I discovered beauty, discovered a way of seeing, and I couldn't change it or make it leave me any more than I could make my father see the harmony of chaos or the power of a single line. What's more, I saw my father not in shades of glory, but in washed tones of reality. He was not the man I wanted to be. He was everything I wouldn't become. In the coming years, my classes would take more field trips to more museums, but I would never match the elation of escape, or the joy of timelessness that found me in the fifth grade. But I would find solitude, and would never lose it.

We had both improved significantly. I had let my guard down considerably since the bathtub date, and was much more comfortable undressing and showing off my body in front of Devin. I also found myself more willing to embrace the learning process without being so self-conscious about what I didn't know. Maggie and I even bought a *Playgirl* magazine and, like two curious teenage girls, sat on the floor of her bedroom and flipped through the pages, gawking at the centerfold. I concluded that Devin, in his Versace suits or in nothing but his silk boxers, still turned me on more than these well-endowed, ripped models. Still, giggling with Maggie and having so much fun karmically resolved the adolescent angst I'd suffered at the hands of Candace.

In turn, Devin was reading and writing on his own in addition to my assignments. Last week, I found a copy of *The Da Vinci Code* on his coffee table, a Marilyn Monroe bookmark wedged neatly somewhere in the middle of the ninth chapter, I guessed (it was the tenth, actually), resting on top of two issues of *The New Yorker*, each dog-ear-flapped to reserve specific articles. His journal entries were longer, less about his dates and more about the things he was doing in his spare time—and lately he'd had more spare time. He was going to museums again—something he used to do when he was in high school and college.

I lost weight. Didn't even notice until Maggie asked me

to attend a meeting with the dean in her place, and my dark gray pinstripe skirt hung loosely around my waist. All the dancing and walking and stretching, I guessed, although I had also failed to realize that I wasn't eating as many sweets anymore, either. The dean (one of Devin's clients) and my other colleagues (also Devin's clients, incidentally—I tried hard to get the image of him bathing their body parts out of my head) noticed my weight loss, however.

"Are you on that low-carb diet?"

"Weight Watchers?"

"Join a gym?"

"New wardrobe? Hairdo?"

But the real culprit revealed itself when Jayce saw Devin and me walking to the Brooklyn Museum of Art one sunny afternoon that week.

"You getting laid, Andi?"

"You getting a life?" I replied.

Brooklyn U was getting in gear for the fall semester, and my department was abuzz with activity, from last-minute class additions and cancellations to schedule rotations, orientation planning, student placement portfolio readings, you name it. Rumors of me being the escort's latest client had circulated faster than the air-conditioning throughout the hallways. I couldn't be sure, but I guessed Jayce had started the grapevine. Only Maggie knew the details of our arrangement, and I implicitly trusted her not to talk; others, however, were less dependable in that regard. When Allison the textbook rep asked me point-blank if I was using Devin's services, I denied it.

"Come on, you don't have to lie. Do you know how many of us there are?" I got the feeling that Allison was really trying to find out exactly what I did with him in order to measure herself against me. I imagined she regretted giving me his card so willingly. Perhaps she wanted him all to herself. Lord knows I did.

"It's none of your business," I replied, my face burning.

———————

Meanwhile, the phone calls between Devin and me went from once a week to three times a week to almost every day, the conversations lasting somewhere between thirty minutes to an hour. The time we spent together in addition to our scheduled meeting days steadily increased as well. Sometimes he'd come out to the Island, and we'd drive out to the East End and tour the vineyards and hop the ferries from Greenport to Shelter Island to Sag Harbor. We found little, secondhand bookstores and could easily spend an hour perusing shelves. We sat in the stands and yelled at the same players and umps during Mets and Yankees games (he was a Mets fan; I was a Yankees fan), and laughed at the same lines on *The Simpsons*.

I reveled in the comforts of his companionship. We never ran out of things to talk about, although we rarely shared anything vulnerably intimate other than what was revealed in our sessions. We platonically related to each other with convenience and ease, despite the romantic and sexual attraction that I so forcefully tried to keep from him (and myself). Even hanging out on the couch watching a movie, brushing up against each other, felt good. It was like dating without the pressure of sex, and for once I wasn't the one calling the shots on whether sex was even going to factor in the equation. This not only relieved me of responsibility but also rendered me powerless to control the situation. The more he educated me about sex, the more I wanted to have it with him, and the more frustrated I grew that he didn't seem to want it with me.

However, I also reveled in, albeit secretly, the one thing that none of his clients were privy to, the one thing that trumped the lack of physical contact: *his attention.* He might be *theirs* for the night, but he called *me* the next day.

Knowing this somehow set me apart from them, yet it also kept me clinging to the hope that eventually things between us would progress.

———

One day at the Brooklyn Museum of Art during a Monet exhibit, I romantically gazed at the garden scenes, while he observed each painting like a scientist observes a phenomenon.

"I absolutely adore the Impressionists," I said dreamily as we moved on to the next painting. Devin stopped in his tracks and shot me a look that screamed absurdity.

"You *what?* You *adore* the Impressionists? No. You can't *adore* them. No one *adores* the Impressionists."

He talked at me with a superior tone while I stood there, unable to comprehend the cardinal sin I'd just committed.

"Why not?"

"You just *don't.* You—no one *adores* them. It can't be done."

"What the hell are you talking about?"

"The Impressionists are *not* 'adorable.' Things that scamper are adorable. Fluffy bunnies hopping in meadows. Little dogs with knitted sweaters. Those little hats that newborns wear. Baby shoes are adorable. Not Impressionists."

"Wha—?"

"You don't 'adore' men who cut off their ears. You don't 'adore' men who eat lead-based paint. Men who refused to compromise themselves or their work, even when it meant depriving their families of food. Men who kept mistresses. Who died poor and alone and bitter. There's something bigger happening in these paintings, something way beyond adoration."

"Don't you think they're beautiful?" I asked, nodding towards the paintings.

"No, I don't. At least not the way *you* think they are." I could feel his words pointing sharply and accusingly at me. "You see pretty things: lilies and bright colors and swirls. Monet was dark and serious."

I listened, unsure of whether to be offended or intrigued.

He continued, "The Impressionists broke all the rules. People weren't supposed to paint like that. But they did what they wanted to do. They poured themselves into the pigment, onto the canvas. It takes great power to paint like that. They're not controlling; they're *harnessing*."

Devin abruptly took me by the wrist and pulled me past a wall of masterpieces, stopping before one of Monet's later works. "Look at this," he commanded, and began a systematic breakdown of the painting's colors, lighting, texture, and composition. "This is dark and intense—you'll never find *this* on a greeting card."

I marveled at it, fascinated by both the painting and his analysis. Indeed, I had never seen Monet—or Devin—in this light. He now stood speechless in front of the painting, still entranced by it. I peered at him from the corner of my eye: he seemed wistful for a moment. I thought about how he'd been discouraged by his father from pursuing his artistic interests, how his father had kicked the passion right out of him. The whole thing had been a rant, a tirade, an explosion of suppressed desire. For that moment, I felt as if I could read his mind, and I fought the urge to slip my hand into his.

"Calendars with pictures of kittens hanging from trees that say, 'Hang in there, baby,' are 'adorable,'" he muttered after a bout of silence. We turned and broke into hushed giggling just as our eyes connected. We moved to the next painting and stood before it in resumed silence together.

And then it occurred to me: neither of us ever dared to admit that we'd broken the rules of our contract.

Because of our demanding schedules the following week, Devin and I had to postpone our final meeting. The English department had its "Welcome Back" faculty orientation (which I single-handedly planned and led this year), followed by drinks at the Heartland Brewery. Jayce, Maggie, and Jonah Stockwell, our recently appointed chairperson, were listening to me and roaring with laughter as I recounted a student's placement essay I'd read about a poor immigrant named Robert (whose name we gave a French pronunciation) who needed to smash a can of corn against the counter to open it because his country was so economically deprived they didn't have can openers; and then, upon arriving in America, he dropped to his knees in thanksgiving for the bounty in the "isle" (I spelled out the word for them) of potato chips—all in response to a prompt about American supermarkets—when I nearly snapped my neck as I caught a glimpse of the Helmut Lang jacket and Gap jeans that had just entered the bar with Della Mason, one of our adjunct faculty members. Della Mason: a pudgy, elfin woman with ash-blond, dyed hair and dark brown-gray roots that grew out to at least an inch long before she got a touch-up. A forty-something who attempted to dress like she was twenty-something and wound up looking fifty-something. A woman who, much to my disdain, called freshman composition classes "Ghetto 101."

I stopped in mid-sentence and froze and clenched my ginger ale glass so tightly it nearly broke in my hands. Maggie, not one for tact, blurted, "Oh my God, Andi—isn't that...your guy...with Della?" She managed to stop herself from calling Devin an escort in front of Jonah, who poorly concealed a glare of judgment at me.

"I don't know what you're talking about, Mags." I attempted to bluff my way through coolly and shot her a look that could've blown a hole in the wall. "I don't have 'a guy.'"

Realizing too late that she'd spoken in front of forbidden company, Maggie tried to backpedal her way out and rescue me. "Of course you don't. I was thinking it was that guy you told me you met last week. You know, the friend of your brother's?"

The damage was already done, though. Besides, by now, everyone knew about Devin the Escort.

"Yeah, right," Jonah snickered under his breath and went to refresh his drink. As he left, Mags turned to me, her face red as merlot, mine pale as chardonnay.

"I am *soooo sorry!* Oh God, I can't believe I said that in front of Jayce and *Jonah!*"

"Fuck it," I snapped and gulped my drink, the carbonation pinching my nostrils and causing me to blink rapidly.

Della had found out about Devin through one of the tenured faculty members, and I guessed this appearance was a sort of self-imposed initiation, a wanting to sit at the grown-up's table. I stared at them venomously, feeling a rage not unlike the first time I saw Andrew and Tanya together in a CVS, waiting in line to buy Robitussin and giving each other congested kisses. When she pulled off her glove to pay for the medicine, I saw the platinum engagement ring catching the glare of the sunlight beaming through the picture window behind the cash wrap counter, like a spotlight just for me. If I could've, I would've jumped and wrestled them both to the ground in a rolling takedown, taken the shaving gel and Gillette Venus razor from my basket, and shaved their heads. But at Heartland, I just remained frozen and shook on the inside.

"Of all people," I muttered. "She still uses red pen and editing symbols on her students' papers. She still makes them read 'Once More to the Lake.' And she's an *adjunct*—hell, she doesn't even get health insurance! How can she afford him?"

"Maybe she's got an arrangement like you do."

"Oh yeah? And what does she teach him—subordinate clauses?"

"Maybe she saved her pennies. Or sold her car."

Despite her attempt to make me laugh and compensate for her earlier blunder, Maggie was only fueling my frustration.

"She's not even good-looking," I said, only to hear Devin's voice echo back in my mind, *All women are beautiful, Andi.*

Fucking rat-bastard.

To add to my mortification, Devin caught a glimpse of me and made eye contact in acknowledgement. He offered to buy Della a drink and left her side to go to the bar, where I was standing at the far end. It was too late for me to pretend I didn't see him or to make a break for it. This was one of those rare moments when I wished I drank—I would've been downing Mike's Hard Lemonade by the case.

"Hey, Andi."

I gave him the same look as I'd given Mags when she swallowed her foot whole.

"Hey."

"What's up?"

"You tell me."

"I'm working. What are you doing?"

"I'm kicking back after a kick-ass orientation."

"So, it went well? That's great. I know you worked hard planning it. Hey, you free tomorrow? That new Woody Allen movie is out, and I thought you'd wanna see it."

Jayce conspicuously listened to every word, while Della

watched him talk to me with the same jealous rage in her eyes as in mine. I darted my eyes to see who was watching and leaned into him.

"Get away from me and don't talk to me for the rest of the night."

"What is wrong with you?"

"I am with my *colleagues* here!"

"Half of whom are my clients, as you probably already know."

"Not me—I am *not* going to be subject to this guilt-by-association. Just go back to your client—who has as much knowledge about rhetoric and composition theory as a rhesus monkey, by the way—and tell her how beautiful she is, 'cause I think she needs to hear it."

His sienna eyes pierced through me, only this time they weren't alluring or consoling, but rather disconcerting, as if to issue a warning.

"I'll call you tomorrow."

Before I could respond, he moved to the other end of the bar and ordered two drinks. Still holding my glass, I drank a few ice chips and crunched forcefully, my whole body trembling from an invisible chill. Jayce sidled over to me and casually draped her arm around my shoulder.

"So—how long has *this* been goin' on?" she asked, her voice light and airy and inoffensive.

"Nothing's goin' on, Jayce."

"Come on! I know you're seeing him!"

"We're just friends, OK?"

"*Friends?*" she gasped, as if the notion were absurd: who befriends an escort?

"Jayce, if you spread this around, so help me, I'll find a way to fuck up your life."

I could almost see my brother Tony in his leather jacket, giving me a thumbs-up approval as if I were standing up to the bully who used to take my milk money. But she wasn't a bully—she was my friend, and she looked hurt.

"Look, there's nothing to be embarrassed about. Actually, I think it's kinda cool that you're—"

"I gotta go…"

I grabbed my purse from the barstool and whisked past the small bunch of Brooklyn University faculty, most of whom were already pretty well soused, and Devin and Della, who had just lit a cigarette and had a look of satisfaction on her face from the mere anticipation of what she was gonna get from him as soon as she could get him out of there.

At that moment, I knew how Allison and Wanda and the others felt (even Della) every time they saw Devin with another woman. All time stopped. The dream was over. Sure, they might exchange knowing glances with each other. They might look unaffected—I was sure they'd learned to fake it and play it cool—but inside, they could not escape their home truths. Inside, they all craved him for themselves. He made us feel special for the moment, and then we saw we weren't all that special after all. And that letdown was worse than if he'd actually been ours in the first place and we'd lost him to another woman. He belonged to no one.

FOURTEEN

D EVIN CALLED ME the next day, keeping his word. I swallowed hard and took in a deep breath before speaking.

"I'm sorry about yesterday," I said.

"It's OK."

"It was the first time I saw you in mixed company since we started this arrangement. It took me by surprise."

"I shouldn't have approached you. It was completely unprofessional of me. I never acknowledge my clients unless they acknowledge me first."

His reference to me as a "client" troubled me. What had we been doing for the last six weeks at his apartment and the last three weeks at museums and coffee bars and bookshops? Surely I couldn't be compared to his other clients. Had I spoken incorrectly when I told Jayce we were friends? There didn't seem to be another word.

I didn't take notice of the silence that dominated the phone line.

"So," he resumed, "you wanna see that movie? Got three and a half stars in *Newsday.*"

I listened to him, baffled. I hadn't expected the phone call, much less the follow-through on the invitation. If anything, I thought he was going to assert that it would be best for us not to see each other anymore, even though we had one meeting left, officially. That we'd both gotten too personal and violated the contract, and rather than pay the fines we should just go our separate ways. Instead, he read off movie times. Geez, he'd even called the theater in advance: he was anticipating us going together—hell, planning it all along, as if I'd never freaked out the day before. I was not accustomed to a man sticking around, especially in the wake of my insecurity.

"Sure," I responded, sounding somewhat dazed.

FIFTEEN

Final Week of the Arrangement

W E HAD CONCLUDED the writing instruction the day before. Devin submitted a final portfolio containing his memoir, the commentary, the literacy narrative I'd assigned him at our first meeting, five journal entries, and a brief reflective essay not unlike the ones I require of my students to submit with their final portfolios.

> I learned that my strength in writing is my patience. I let the process guide me rather than trying to force something to happen. And yet, I'm often surprised by what comes out. Oftentimes it takes a couple of drafts for me to uncover what I really want to say. I like being descriptive and using imagery. Language is not unlike art in that words contain values of lights and darks, hues and tonalities, texture and sensuality. Words can paint complex pictures.
>
> My weakness would have to be writing persuasively. Again, I think this has to do with taking time to uncover my meaning. By the time I find my claim and get to the point, I've distracted the reader with information not necessarily pertinent to the argument

itself. I am certain that by studying more examples and with practice, I could improve. I also want to improve my critical reading of a text, much like I can do with a visual.

The pleasant surprise is how much I enjoyed myself and the process. I'm reading a lot more (although, I have to admit, the Greek classics were not my taste—perhaps I'll try the Romans sometime), and I noticed I'm seeing things differently. That's something I never would've expected. Not only that, but I'm thinking about what I'm seeing. I also recalled a lot of memories—some pleasant, some not so pleasant, that offered a new perspective. I understand context so much more now. Overall, I think I did well, and I'm grateful to have had a teacher who was thoughtful, challenging, and talented.

I could almost see him winking at me as I read the last words. In response, I wrote a final evaluation to him:

Devin,

This portfolio demonstrates that you've not only accomplished a variety of writing tasks, but that you are able to adapt your writing voice and style to accommodate your purpose and/or audience. I am particularly impressed by your use of metaphor and description. Your descriptions are detailed, your words energetic, your sentences rhythmic; each of these elements paint a panoramic view of meaning. You also have an excellent command of vocabulary. I like your voice.

I agree with your self-assessment regarding argument; however, you've shown me that you take time to think about your topic, and you have an ability to see multiple sides of an issue. Your journal pieces get better and better—you have a knack for recalling details and a critical eye, no doubt the result of your art training (the account of the Matisse exhibit read much like a review to me). Overall, you've embraced the concept of revision as a process that is constantly unfolding and nonlinear. You've been open to the process, willing to explore, and I derive so much pleasure from seeing the results of that willingness on the page. Indeed, you are a *writer*.

My "final" was a date with Devin the Escort. We met at night and at my place, and he instructed me to wear something sexy. The week before, I blew over two hundred dollars on satin and lace bras, panties, teddies, hosiery, and vanilla body lotion at Victoria's Secret. I opened the door to see him in his usual Versace, and I saw his eyes immediately scan the black cocktail dress and thigh-high sheers I was wearing. My feet were already killing me in three-inch, sling-back heels. With that one look, he gasped and exclaimed, "*Bellisima!*" blowing an Italian kiss with his fingers while his eyes shot off fireworks.

I beamed.

He brought chilled sparkling cider and strawberries in sterling silver buckets and set them out for me. I carefully sipped the cider from a crystal Mikasa flute and dipped one of the strawberries in a bowl of melted chocolate. The sensation of the flavors mixing in my mouth shot currents down my back.

"You know," he started, "I always meant to ask: how come you don't drink?"

"I can't stomach it," I replied. "Like the way some people are with dairy."

"Do you miss it?"

"Alcohol? Never."

"How come?"

"I never liked it. I've been in too many bars and clubs, watching my brothers perform, to see its effects, not to mention knowing some once-brilliant professors whose intellects have just withered away in the slosh of booze. It's sad, really."

"Hmm."

We danced to Diana Krall's cover of "The Look of Love" saying little, if anything, to each other. Even in my heels, I could just about reach around his shoulders, and I let my hands touch his hair at the nape of his neck while his hands brushed the small of my back like feathers. We locked in to each other's gaze, and the world disappeared. Then Devin took me by the hand and led me to my bedroom. I had changed the bulbs in the reading lamps to soft pink, and bought creamy, fine percale sheets at Linens 'n Things. Vanilla-scented votives burned unobtrusively on the dresser and nightstand and next to my reading chair.

"Nice," he approved, scanning the room.

He dipped and practically dropped me on the bed. By now the mantra was *have no fear*. Men like women who are neither too timid nor too forceful, who like to play, who aren't obsessing over their bodies. Just relax and have fun.

"Close your eyes," he instructed.

I did so.

"OK: open them now." When I did, I spied a white box with a red ribbon wrapped around it, in his hand, extended to me.

I took the box, pulled off the ribbon, and opened it. Then I looked at it, then him, incredulously.

It was plastic and smooth and had a leopard skin pattern. It required two C batteries. It stood tall and erect, and a condom could easily slip on and off it.

"Do you like it?" he asked.

"I'm...a bit...surprised," I stammered.

"Haven't you ever used a vibrator before?"

I didn't respond.

"Haven't you ever *seen* one?"

I raised my eyebrows.

"Well, this one's for you. I thought you'd like the leopard skin." He winked.

I did. I removed it from the box and turned it on. The vibe made a soft, purring noise.

"The batteries are included," he remarked.

"What, no blinking lights? Does it also talk dirty to you?"

"No, but it'll call you tomorrow."

Devin turned out the lights and blew out all the candles except two. He switched the CD from Diana Krall to Tchaikovsky's *Swan Lake* (they were both on my list of music that gets me in the mood). I stretched out on the bed, resting on my elbow. He sat on the bed next to me.

"Take off your shoes," he commanded. I loosened each sling-back with my foot and flung them off, one by one. He ran his fingers up my thigh and pulled each of the sheers down, one by one. He then unzipped and removed my dress, letting the fabric of my black satin, spaghetti-strapped slip slide along my skin, revealing satin, leopard skin print bikini panties.

"Hey, they match!" he said, holding the vibrator next to the print. I tossed my head back and laughed freely, flirtatiously.

I started to sit up and wrap my arms around his shoulders and neck, but he took them away and gently pushed me so that I fell on my back, my head on the pillow. I could barely hear the music in the background, even though the volume was up. In a seemingly involuntary motion, I pressed my lips to his. He stopped me and fed me a strawberry instead, and then gave me a piece of cider-soaked ice to suck on. But this didn't satisfy me; I spat out the ice cube, shooting it against the wall, and kissed him again. This time, he gave in, swirling his tongue around mine. Finally. Oh God, it felt good—in fact, I don't remember a kiss ever feeling quite so...*lascivious.* His lips felt smooth and firm and moist all at the same time. We kissed some more, and I ran my fingers through his hair as he climbed on top of me and pinned me on the bed. I breathed heavily.

He slowly lowered my bikinis and moved his hands around my waist, careful not to tickle me, showing me how to move. "Think of dancing," he whispered. "Relax." As he began to kiss my neck, a deluge of repressed memories rushed and submerged me in an instant:

. . . I am nine years old and announce that I am going to marry Shaun Cassidy. My brothers laugh at and tease me. "Why would Shaun Cassidy want to marry you? You're only nine." "He'll wait for me," I insist. "He doesn't even know

you exist," Joey says. My father interjects: "You're not marrying anyone. *For crying out loud, do you even know what you're saying?"*

. . . I am ten years old and dress my Barbie doll in Daisy Duke shorts and a halter top, and do the best I can to position her and Ken's straight and stiff joints to hug and make out with each other. My mother sees this and reprimands me. "Play with your baby dolls instead." "I don't like them," I respond. "Then play something else. And change her clothes—she looks like a hooker." I don't know what a "hooker" is, but from the tone of her voice, I know it's something bad. I look down to notice that I too am wearing cutoffs and a halter top . . .

. . . I am eleven and my parents are in the den watching the miniseries The Thorn Birds. *I wander in, my math book in tow, and sit on the couch. I've walked in on Rachel Ward seducing her Australian lover in the pond. I watch with curiosity. My father erupts: "Do you know what she's doing? She's* giving herself *to this man!" I don't know what "giving herself" means. He continues to holler at me for watching the lurid scene, for being in the room in the first place, for Rachel Ward's promiscuity. My mother defends my naïveté, and my parents begin arguing. I leave the room dejected and sick to my stomach, math book in tow, never getting the help with my homework. In my room, I shudder with shame—I actually liked "giving herself" . . .*

Tears spilled down my cheeks, leaving lines in my makeup along my face, and dropped onto the new percale pillow. "Devin, stop . . ."

He stopped and looked at me.

"I can't," I cried. "I just can't. Oh God."

"Why not?"

"I've never actually done it."

He sat up, a bit startled at first.

"What?" he asked more out of shock than incoherence.

"I mean, I've done stuff with guys. You know, hand jobs and that sort of thing." I felt stupid saying the words *hand jobs*. "But I never went all the way."

"Are you telling me you're a virgin?"

"I decided a long time ago that I would wait until I got married—that that was the romantic thing to do. I didn't even date until I was twenty—between my father's death and my brothers' overprotection and the yo-yoing with my weight, there was no other chance. The first guy I was ever with told me I was a disappointment. He said he'd had better. He told me I was too 'Catholic schoolgirl' because I didn't know anything and because I wanted to wait."

"What an asshole," Devin responded. "I'm so sorry you believed him."

"After that, I changed my mind and decided not to wait. I wanted to learn, but I was too embarrassed, too afraid someone would find out that I didn't know what I was doing."

"So you didn't have intercourse with any of the guys you dated?"

"I wanted to, lots of times, especially with Andrew. God, I loved Andrew more than any of 'em. But every time I tried, something stopped me, and I couldn't go through with it. As a result, my relationships never lasted beyond a few months. Except for Andrew. When he came along, at first I changed my mind again and told him I wanted to wait until we were married, and he agreed to that. He loved me a lot, and I was certain he was 'the one.' But we were both getting restless. I thought I'd get comfortable in time. I thought my inexperience and the insecurity that came with it would go away. It never did, though, and the more time that passed, the more afraid I became that I couldn't actually go through with it. Every time I tried, I froze. Eventually, Andrew started telling me that I didn't please him. He kept telling me that what I didn't know was a hindrance. I tried to please him, I really did. I just didn't know how. I mean, how was I supposed to know?"

Devin finally interrupted my rambling. "It's OK." He said it again, rubbing my shoulder and arm. "Andi, it's OK."

"It's not OK!" I protested. "I'm thirty-four years old!"

"So? What's wrong with that?"

"Everything!"

"Says who? Andrew? And who is he—Professor Wonderstud?"

"Every guy I've ever been with eventually left me because they were either turned off or unsatisfied, even if I tried to fake it or say I didn't want to or wasn't ready."

"How many guys have there been?"

I paused to take a quick mental survey.

"Including Andrew? Five. Although one of them only lasted for two weeks…"

"Did they specifically tell you that that was the reason why they broke up with you?"

"Not all of them."

"Then you can't make that claim. False logic. Polarization."

"Devin—" I started.

"Andi!" He cupped his hands around my chin. Then he

spoke more softly, with tenderness. "Andrea." He looked into my eyes, and I suddenly felt as if I were looking at a different person. And yet, this person was warm and loving and safe. I babbled out the repressed memories, one by one. He listened patiently and compassionately, caressing my cheek intermittently. Finally he stopped me.

"Listen to me: there is nothing wrong with you. Do you hear me? Look at me: there is *nothing wrong* with you. You think the fact that you never had intercourse has been the problem all this time? That was *never* the problem—the problem all these years was neither your inhibition nor your inexperience. It was your *shame*. And there was nothing to be ashamed of. For God's sake, your family guilted you into suppressing your sexuality, and for no good reason. No matter what choice you made, you couldn't win. If you expressed yourself, if you 'gave yourself' to someone you loved, you'd be degraded. And yet, you were also given the message that you weren't worth waiting for. Add that to all the times your brothers said hands off... I mean, geez, Andi. If anyone's to be ashamed, it's *them*. Fuck 'em all—how dare they do that to you! They were wrong. They misled you."

His words soaked into my skin and circulated through my blood like an antibiotic, cleansing and washing away every prudish prevarication that imprisoned my innocence. He cupped my face again, his own eyes glassy.

"My God, Andi. You're so beautiful. All of you. You are a vibrant, passionate woman with abounding creativity and wisdom and humor. You are enticing and delectable. You have a body that is a joy to explore, a rapture to the senses. You smell and taste and look and feel and sound good. And above all, you are sexual. Always were. You don't need sex to be sexual. Never did."

No one, not even Andrew, had ever said such things to me before. And for the first time, I believed every word. Devin held me while I wept, rubbing my back and stroking my hair. As I quieted, he dried my tears, careful not to smudge my makeup. He kissed me first on my forehead, then on my cheek. But this time he was the one who seemed dissatisfied, and kissed my lips softly. And it was he who didn't stop. I kept kissing him and leaned back and pulled him on top of me.

He stopped for a moment and looked at me. "You're a good kisser," he said softly. Then he whispered in my ear, "Andrew was a fool to let you go."

"I'm ready now," I said with an acceptance and affirmation in my voice I'd never heard before. Devin blew out the last two votives, picked up the vibrator, and turned it on again.

Something with a parasitic appetite left me that night and never returned, washed away with the river of tears, leaving a soothing, fountain-like serenity in its place.

I still blush when I think of the things he was able to do with that vibrator, and the way it made me feel. And now, whenever I hear *Swan Lake*, I am conditioned to the sound of soft buzzing in Pavlovian fashion, and must splash some cold water on my face.

SIXTEEN

October

I HAD FALLEN IN LOVE with Devin. Duh.

It probably started that day we danced stripped down in his apartment over the summer. Or maybe even sooner, I don't know. It took some time for me to admit. But my eyes lit up when he entered a room, and my heart leapt when he ran even just a finger down my arm. The unexpected friendship confused things even more. Our contract had explicitly stated that we were not to get so personal that romantic feelings would evolve, but the platonic relationship had broken that rule, and neither of us had ever held the other accountable for it.

The fall semester had begun, and I entered my classes with an unexpected renewal, excited about the coming weeks. I could feel a bounce in my step, a lighter laugh, a feeling of having dropped a bag of heavy rocks I'd been carrying around my entire life. And my new students seemed attuned to this energy. They were just as eager as I was to come to class, to write, to learn something. Outside of class, the faculty meetings were livelier than ever, with Maggie and me working more as codirectors than director and assistant.

Andrew was fading like a photo in the sun.

And yet, still…something wasn't quite right.

"You look fantastic," Maggie remarked one day over lunch. "Your skin is glowing."

"Yeah, well, not for long."

"Why?" She leaned in and whispered, "You're not *pregnant*, are you?"

"Geez, no—it's nothing like that. I told you, we haven't actually slept together—well…oh hell, you know what I mean. It's just that I've fallen in love with this guy and there's no chance of us getting together."

"Why not? You're spending time with him, aren't you? In fact, it seems to me that you're *dating* him. How many clients does he go to the movies with on his day off?"

"Mags, he's an *escort*. This wasn't the arrangement we had. We violated the terms of our contract."

"I thought the contract ended."

"It did. But we broke it before it ended."

"And whose fault is that?"

"Hard to tell. Anyway, we're both responsible, I guess. I mean, we should both pay up."

"Maybe he has feelings for you," she said.

"Maybe not," I replied.

"Maybe you should find out."

"Maybe I shouldn't."

———

My feelings for Devin were obvious, but neither of us said a word about them. After the "final," we continued to see each other as friends, meeting for coffee or going to museums or out to dinner. He even came to my apartment a few times to watch a movie or a Yankee game. By this time, we were quite comfortable with each other—to the point of finishing each other's sentences—but he kept me in check when I tried to hold his hand or flirt with him. He was used to that. Business as usual, even after our contract expired and our arrangement officially ended. We never talked about that final night, or my revelation. And although he would occasionally kiss me on the cheek, he wouldn't dare let me kiss him, ever. It frustrated me to no end that he showered me with so much attention yet restrained himself—and me—from so much emotional affection. How could he be like that? I wondered. Of all the women he'd serviced in the last five years, did he manage never to fall in love with even one? How?

I got up the nerve to ask him while walking through Central Park one afternoon.

"I simply told myself not to," he answered. "It's a matter of ethics. Think of your students. How would you respond if I asked you if you ever fell in love with one of them?"

"That's different."

"How? You offer them a service. They're part of your working environment."

"Yeah, but I don't teach them to write while rubbing whipped cream on their nipples and licking it off."

"But you make them get naked every day. Come on, Andi. There is nothing more vulnerable to those kids than to put their thoughts on paper and have you evaluate them. You know that. They want you to like what they write. They wanna walk away feeling better about themselves. So tell me how that's different. And you're just as professional about your work as I am about mine, and you're just as good at what you do as I am at what I do. You wouldn't compromise that."

I said nothing in response. Instead, I walked pensively before continuing the interrogation.

"Are you ever sexually attracted to a client? Have you ever gotten aroused?"

"Sure, lots of times."

I remembered our foreplay lesson, the bathtub date, and the night of the final, in that order. I wanted to ask, "With me?" but was too afraid his response would be "Hell no" followed by "Are you kidding me?" Instead, I pressed on.

"Whaddya do?"

"I take a cold shower or whack off like any other guy."

"You're so fucking poetic," I said. "And you're telling me that you never once let them..." I tried to finish the sentence, but couldn't. Instead, I raised my eyebrows at him.

"Not if I can help it. It's not in the contract."

Of course it wasn't in the fucking contract. I wanted to point accusingly and say, *A-ha!* Instead, I said, "So, you've not had sex all this time?"

"I didn't say that. I get laid—maybe not as often as I'd like to, but I do. Just not with my clients, that's all."

"You've *never* slept with any of your clients? Never went all the way, never got paid for it? Never did it with them for free?"

"I told you, *never.*"

"Then with whom?"

"Women I meet at clubs or galleries or parties when I'm not working."

I looked away from him, my brows turned inward, dismayed. When was the last time he'd done it? Was it recently and he didn't tell me? What did she look like?

"Do you call these women the next day?"

"Not usually. Sometimes."

"Do they call you?"

"We have an understanding that's it's not a long-term thing."

"Do you tell them you're an escort?"

"Sometimes."

"What do they say?"

"It's a turn-on."

I scoffed, "I'll bet."

———

At Borders, while he flipped through the pages of a book about Van Gogh, I approached him and leaned in.

"Do you kiss your clients?" I asked.

"I don't initiate it, if that's what you mean," he answered, still looking at the book.

"But you let them kiss you. Totally make out with you."

"If that's what they want, yeah."

"How come you stop me?"

"It's different with you."

"How?"

"It just is."

"That's a stupid answer."

"It's the only one you're gonna get," he said, annoyed.

Frustrated, I headed to the chick lit section while he finished Van Gogh and picked up Mondrian.

Later, while sitting in Café Dante, I asked him yet another question between sips of mochaccino.

"So, when was the last time you were in a serious love relationship?" I asked.

"Couple of years ago, I think. Before the business took off. I haven't had much time for a personal life."

"You make time for me."

"That's different."

"How?" I asked more emphatically than the last time.

"We're not dating."

The reality of the words hit me like a wave and almost knocked me over. I had to look down in order to hide the disappointment in my eyes. I felt like I'd been smacked.

"What's the difference?" I asked.

"A love relationship is more work. It takes more time and energy. I love pleasing my clients, but sometimes it completely wears me out, both physically and mentally. Some of them are so needy. They've just been so neglected, either by themselves or their husbands or whoever. To go through all of that night after night, listening to them and touching them, and then have to attend to my girlfriend? Besides, what girlfriend would be so accepting of my line of work? How does she introduce me to her family?"

"Small business owner in the service industry?"

He cocked his eyebrow.

"Well come on, Dev, it's not like you face the same stigma as I would if *I* were an escort."

"Are you kidding?"

"From whom?"

"My family, for one. Most of them have stopped speaking to me because of my work. Hell, my father's convinced I'm nothing but a pimp and a drug dealer."

The information silently disturbed me, but I pressed on in a cold manner.

"But overall, you make out OK. I mean, I've seen you at work. You talk it up with everyone, whether they're in academia or advertising. I've seen you hand out your business cards with no shame. You represent yourself very well."

"I have a lot of confidence."

"And social support…" I muttered.

Devin frowned. "What's that supposed to mean?"

"It's not fair," I said.

"What's not fair?"

"Men are *escorts*, but women are *hookers*. Men are *studs*, but women are *sluts*. Men are exonerated if caught in adultery, but women are stoned to death. Men are pro-creators, while women are used goods. No matter what, society shames women when it comes to sex, married or single, motherhood or—God help her—childless, in love or not. And virginity is a double-edged sword, too. A man's a champion if he loses his virginity; a woman's 'de-flowered.' Come on! We're pressured to lose it, but once we do, we're considered untouchable because we've 'given it up.' And then if we hold on to it, we're considered prudes, prisses, frigid, or simply freaks of nature. And still untouchable. Did you ever see the *Seinfeld* episode when Jerry dates the virgin? They made her timid as hell. And they labeled her: *Marla the Virgin*. How ostracizing can you get?"

He stared at his empty coffee cup, then looked up at me. "What do you want me to say?"

"I want you to admit that you've got it made, buddy. No one calls you a prostitute. I mean, you don't even have to worry about getting arrested."

"That's because I don't go all the way with these women."

"Oh, *come on*, Dev! Just because you use a vibrator instead? They didn't buy Clinton's definition of sex either."

He smirked. I continued, unamused.

"And don't get me started with domination and abuse. You don't have to worry about getting slapped around, berated, or being judged on every little speck of cellulite that shows or gray hair that appears on your head—"

"But I do have to worry about women stalking or harassing me, or getting the shit kicked out of me by a husband or two. And all of the above has happened. Do you know you're the only person who's been to my apartment since I started working? I've moved twice and changed my phone number three times in the last two years. Hell, Devin's not even my real name…"

I raised my eyebrows at this confession. "It's not?" I asked, under my breath, somewhat bewildered, while he finished his rant.

"So don't tell me about fair. We've all got a burden to carry."

"Then why don't you quit?"

He rolled his eyes. "Here we go…"

"No, I mean it. If it's that bad, then why don't you quit?"

"Because I love my work."

"Oh, that's right," I started, the sarcasm dripping off my tongue like saliva. "It's all about the women. You're Captain Orgasm, rescuing us from the villains of neglect and abandonment and lands of Uglisville and Bad Sex. And you get paid a shitload for this! You know, I'm starting to think that that's what you tell yourself to justify and hide the fact that you're afraid of a serious relationship."

"You think so."

"As Devin the Escort, you get to go on exciting dates. You show up with your cheap smiles and your Versace suits. Then, you haul ass outta there just as they start to get attached. No commitments, no sending roses the next day, no follow-up phone calls. No getting to the real you. Minimal investment, minimal risk. Do you honestly think these women aren't falling in love with you just because you tell them not to, just because you dictate it in writing? Trust me, they are—they're so hooked in and they're too afraid to either admit it or get out, because some desperate part of them is hoping you'll actually fall in love with them and leave the rest behind. You're naïve if you think otherwise."

"I think they stay because they get something out of it. They get a payoff."

"And what about *your* payoff? Sure, you may dance around in your boxers, but have you ever told a woman how you really feel about art or your father or growing older or anything else? Have you ever let yourself be vulnerable to a woman, tell her, even show her you're scared or hurt or angry?"

"Oh, you're a fine one to talk. Look at *you*, Andi. You're one of those needy women! *You're my client.* 'Show me how to be a better lover, Devin.' 'Make me feel less self-conscious, Devin.' 'Men reject me, Devin.' 'I'm undesirable.' What, you think just because you didn't pay me money, just because our arrangement was more intellectual, that that makes you better than them? Maybe if you didn't act so goddamn smug and superior, you'd hold on to a man. And speaking of which, when was the last time *you* got laid by something not requiring batteries? For all your increased confidence and your new clothes and your trimmer body, I don't see any men banging down your door, or banging you, either. Why is that? Maybe your problem wasn't sex, Andi. Maybe it had nothing to do with your body or your upbringing. Maybe Andrew just wasn't that into *you*. After all, he married someone else, didn't he? So don't sit there and preach to me about my relationships until you get one of your own that lasts."

We both looked at each other, shell-shocked.

Unable to refrain from crying, I stood up and ran out of the café, grabbing my jacket but forgetting my purse. Devin picked it up and ran after me, calling my name. I didn't want to stop, didn't want to look at him, but I needed my purse to get back to the Island. I stopped and turned around, but looked at the ground as I held out my hand.

"I'm so sorry," he said.

"Just give me the bag." I lifted my head enough to grab it from his hand, turned, and walked away quickly, not looking back, while fumbling through my purse for a tissue. I heard him call out my name at least one more time, and then the indifference of Manhattan filled my ears yet again.

He was right, and I knew it. And yet, so was I; I was hooked in good, and I'd managed to fool myself along with everyone else.

I sat by the window on the train, leaning against it, crying, while all of Long Island ignored me.

How I missed New England in the fall.

SEVENTEEN

T HE NEXT MORNING, I found a bouquet of a single
white rose surrounded by two dozen red roses at my
doorstep, and a card:

Andi—

*I sank lower than whale shit at the bottom of the ocean yester-
day, and today my sorrow expands to the edges of the universe.
Forgive me, please.*

—Devin

His choice of metaphors was corny as hell. I couldn't
help but smile, although my heart slumped in my chest.
Later that day, I text-messaged him without abbreviating:
All is forgiven.

What I didn't know was that he had canceled his client
last night, and for the next two nights afterwards.

One of the roses wilted over the side of the vase. It
was the first to be removed.

EIGHTEEN

Three Months Later

J ANUARY DAYS ARE gray days. Gray skies, gray grass, gray trees. Leftover gray rock salt and sand litters the sides of gray roads, while mounds of dirty, gray snow linger in gray parking lots. The sun hides under its gray covers, in its own gray slump. Dark, empty gray mornings blend into dark, empty gray afternoons, which quickly fade into dark, empty gray nights.

January days are gray days.

It was on one of those days when I walked out of Penn Station and onto an uncharacteristically sparse Thirty-fourth Street, on my way to this year's Language Arts Conference at the Hilton New York on West Fifty-second Street and Sixth Avenue. In addition to the paper I was presenting on the social rhetorical response of personal essays (I was part of a panel with Maggie and Jayce), I had secretly lined up three interviews: two with universities in the New England area, and one in San Diego. Even Mags didn't know that I'd spent Thanksgiving break searching Listserv databases for job postings and updating my curriculum vitae, and Christmas break e-mailing CVs and returning phone calls from committee chairs to schedule interviews at the conference and checking out the universities' Web sites. Each potential position was for a writing program director. And with Mags's and my textbook set for release in the fall, my prospects looked promising.

Devin had come up with the book's title. We were walking in the MOMA one rainy autumn afternoon, looking at a Picasso painting, when I blurted, "Art is a lie that makes us realize the truth."

"Where'd you hear that?" Devin asked.

"It's a Picasso quote, but I read it at the beginning of Chaim Potok's novel *My Name Is Asher Lev*."

"Yeah, I know it's Picasso. Do you agree with it?"

"Sure do," I said.

"Why?"

"All art, be it writing, painting, film, dance, whatever, is a manipulation of time and space. It's an interpretation and a recreation of the facts, using various artifacts that point us in the direction of our personal truths."

"Not the artist's truth?"

"More so our own. For example: remember the Lad Tobin essay I told you about, the one about Pogo the clown scaring the crap out of him when he was five years old and his parents having to call off the rest of the birthday party? He couldn't actually remember the name of the clown, so he made one up. And remember Patricia Hampl's essay 'Memory and Imagination'? The Thompson piano book, Sister Olive who looked like an olive, Mary Katherine Reilly—all lies, all artifacts that point us to a more personal truth: in the first case, a child's trauma. In the second, envy and insecurity."

"But that's Tobin's trauma, yes? His truth. And Hampl's."

"OK, now think of Donald Murray's 'Onions and Oranges' essay. Murray says that as we read someone else's story, fiction or non, we read—and consequently, we write—our own. In other words, all writing is auto-biographical. Tobin's trauma with Pogo the clown takes me back to me shrieking and begging my mother to take me out of Debbie Doherty's birthday party because there were balloons all over the place and the kids were kicking and popping them. That's *my* truth."

"But was her name *really* Debbie Doherty?" he asked coyly.

I slid my eyes in his direction, cocking an eyebrow, as if to say, *Wouldn't you like to know.*

He flashed his electric smile and winked. "You win this one."

We parked ourselves in front of a Jackson Pollock and stood still for a minute.

"How's the textbook coming along?" he asked, still looking at the painting.

"Mags is filling in some of the missing research, and I'm doing revisions. We've also got to finish the introduction and the last two chapters."

"Hm."

We stared at the painting. Then he turned to me.

"What's the title?"

"This Book Sucks."

A guffaw escaped from him, echoed on the other side of the room, and drew irked expressions in our direction from wandering patrons. He covered his mouth quickly and stifled the rest of his laughter.

"Actually, we can't decide on a title. We vacillate from too stuffy and academic to too cutesy."

"Hm."

We moved to the next Pollock, stood, and stared at it in silence. He turned to me again.

"How about 'Truth, Lies, and Artifacts'?"

Do you know the satisfaction, the elation one gets when fitting the final piece into a jigsaw puzzle? It was absolutely perfect; it fit so well, completing the entire picture. There could be no other title. And I was mad as hell that I hadn't thought of it myself.

"You rat-bastard," I said under my breath, still looking at the painting.

"You're welcome," he replied. A proud grin pushed out the corners of his mouth as we turned to each other and locked into a gaze that revealed the kind of connection that happens between two people who know each other really well. Was it the connection of friends? Lovers? I couldn't be sure. I'd never had it before with anyone. Not even Andrew.

His goofy grin spread to my own face, and my eyes glistened. We kept looking at each other.

"What's your real name?" I asked.

He hesitated for a moment.

"David."

"David what?"

"David Santino."

He was Italian.

"Hm," I said.

We moved on to the next painting.

The holidays were Devin's busiest time of year; often he had two or three dates on the same day—an office Christmas party in the afternoon, a cocktail party in the early evening, and a play or ballet at night. One night during the week before Christmas, he called me at two o'clock in the morning.

"If I have to see the fucking *Nutcracker* one more time, I swear I'm gonna have a seizure." He didn't even say hello.

"Could be worse," I said groggily. "Could be the *Magnificent Christmas Spectacular* at Radio City. Real, live camels taking a dump on stage, fortunately *after* the Rockettes do their wooden solider routine. Or maybe unfortunately, if you're not a fan of the Rockettes."

He cracked up. "You always make me feel better."

"Good. Now let me get some sleep."

My datebook wasn't exactly blank, either. I attended party after party, went Christmas shopping, caught a show with Maggie and Jayce, and even went on a date with a guy I met at a Christmas cocktail party for writing program directors in Port Washington, hosted by Westford-Langley publishers. Carol had introduced me to him. Seemed OK at the time. Nice. Friendly. Salt-and-pepper hair. Brown eyes. Five o'clock shadow. Bit of a pudge. His name was Bob.

We went out for dinner the next night at the Cheesecake Factory in Garden City. His choice.

Bob directed the writing program at Long Island Community College. Bob wore a tie with cartoon Santas on them, and confessed that his boxer shorts matched. Bob drank Bacardi with a twist, and asked me if I was a friend of Bill W. when I told him I didn't drink. Bob had two Bacardis with a twist before dinner and a brandy after dinner. Bob had a PhD in literature and thus re-instilled literature in the writing curriculum at LICC. "They'll never pick up another book again otherwise," said Bob. "Why, what do you teach at Brooklyn U?"

"Oh, we've adapted more of a hybrid of public and personal writing with an emphasis on rhetoric, and portfolio assessment."

Bob shook his head as he finished his brandy. "Portfolios—too much work."

I nodded, my lips pressed together. Then I excused myself to go to the ladies' room and called Maggie.

"Get me the hell out of here."

When I got back to the table, Bob looked at the dessert menu. "By the way, are we going dutch on this?" he asked.

My cell phone rang; it was Maggie conjuring a fake emergency of being stranded in her car on the Verrazano Bridge—she even acted it out by calling me outside on Flatbush Avenue in case Bob could hear her and the traffic over the phone. Still, he looked at me, and the phone, suspiciously.

"Sorry," I said, picking up my coat. "I've gotta go. Thanks, though. Merry Christmas." Fortunately, I'd driven myself there.

"No dessert? I thought you said you loved cheesecake."

"Once you've had Junior's, everything else pretty much tastes ordinary."

I stuck Bob with the check and left, not before I cornered the server and told him to delay giving Bob the check as long as possible so he wouldn't drive drunk.

It was the first real date I'd been on since Andrew and I broke up. How sad.

Devin gave himself Christmas Eve off, and he and I exchanged gifts before going our separate ways to our respective families' homes on the Island. I gave him a journal from the MOMA gift store, with a leather spine and Matisse reproduction on the cover, as well as a matching Cross pen. "I thought of you when I saw it," I said of the journal, afraid he'd think it was one step above a kitten calendar. He was visibly and genuinely moved, however.

"I love it," he said. "Thank you." He kissed me on the cheek.

He gave me an elegant mahogany statue of a woman, her voluptuous body sensually posed. Its box had a gold seal on top, marking the name of one of the many galleries we'd visited. "It's a one-of-a-kind piece," he said. "Made me think of you."

I drew in a breath and could barely get the words "thank you" out. My heart felt as heavy as a rock. I had resigned myself some time ago to the fact that we were never going to be anything more than friends, and had given up on the idea of telling him how I really felt about him. What was the point? If he'd felt otherwise, he would've told me and we'd be ending our get-togethers by going to bed rather than getting on the train. Besides, I figured he'd always known I was in love with him. It was the one thing I couldn't fake, no matter how hard I tried.

But it didn't ease the disappointment, especially as I held that delicate statue in my hands.

We parted company with an extended embrace.

———

I shivered as I walked for almost ten blocks before finally hailing a cab successfully.

Once at the hotel, I attended my interviews in the morning and presented my paper in the afternoon following lunch with Jayce (we were both so nervous that we could barely swallow a few spoonfuls of soup). Both the interviews and my presentation went well, even when one of my pages slid off the podium and floated like a carefree leaf onto the floor. I improvised for a bit, leaving the fallen page where it landed, and picked up at the next page without missing a beat.

Cocktail parties hosted by textbooks companies abounded for the duration of the conference, and I was certain Devin would appear at any one of them as Allison's or someone else's escort. I should've gone to as many of these events as possible to network and plug our forthcoming book, but I steered clear, even when Maggie called me from one and said that she ran into Devin and he seemed to be looking for me. I could no longer stomach seeing him with other women—especially women I knew—imagining him running his hands up and down their thighs or their backs or feeding them strawberries and champagne or bringing them to dizzying heights of ecstasy. *Kissing* them. And I noticed that he'd all but stopped talking to me about work, especially since my meltdown at Heartland Brewery months ago.

On the last day of the conference, as Maggie and I checked out the schedule, my mouth dropped open when I saw one of the eleven o'clock sessions. "Unplugged: Folk Tales and the Composition Classroom," to be presented by Andrew and Tanya Clark. Bride and groom. I nudged Maggie and pointed to the program.

"Folk Boy's at it again, and he's doing a duet now."

"You should go!" Maggie said.

I looked at her incredulously.

"No, really! You look so good, and he'll see that you've moved on."

A series of five-second fantasies sequenced through my mind: me showing up in a low-cut red dress and stiletto heels, sitting smack in the middle of the room and sucking on a watermelon-flavored Jolly Rancher, driving him to distraction; me standing in the back of the room and heckling him by holding up and waving a Bic lighter, yelling, *Freebird!*"; me sneaking into the room beforehand and fudging with the Power Point equipment; me asking him a question that was sure to stump him: *Aren't you pigeonholing students to a limited genre of writing that doesn't lend itself to a more traditional curriculum?* A bullshit question, but sure to stump him.

I opted to go to a different session.

It was called "Homeward Bound: A Return to the Expressivists in the 21st Century," and one of the panel speakers was Sam Vanzant, a professor at Edmund College in Amherst, not far from Northampton University, one of the three places for which I'd just interviewed. I'd read (and liked) several of his articles in *The Journal of College Writing* when I was still a PhD student, but never saw him in person. When he stepped up to the podium, I recognized him as one who'd attended my session two days ago.

I'd had difficulty focusing my attention during the first

two speakers before him, still hyperaware that Andrew—or Tanya—was speaking in an adjacent room. Dr. Vanzant, however, reeled me in and made me forget about Andrew altogether. He was extremely handsome: high, defined cheekbones; deep blue eyes; short, tapered haircut; and tall frame. Very Rob Lowe. I couldn't be sure, but I thought he smiled whenever he looked in my direction. And he seemed to be looking in my direction quite a bit.

During the Q&A, an attendee asked about pliability in the classroom using the modes of discourse (which sounded a lot like my fantasy bullshit question to Andrew). I was busy scribbling notes on my pad, *again with the fucking modes* being one of them.

"Actually, I think Doctor Cutrone can answer that question, since she delivered a paper this week about rhetoric and the personal essay," he said.

He gestured towards me, and all heads turned to meet my deer-in-the-headlights expression. I dropped my pen, which made an amplified clacking dance on the hardwood floor (the only one not carpeted, of course), only to be followed by the thumping and swishing sounds of my water bottle (closed, thank God) when I knocked it over in an attempt to retrieve the pen. Maggie was next to me, beaming, and chimed, "Yeah, Andi, tell 'em!"

"Well, for starters…" I stalled, then drew in a breath. "My paper was about social rhetorical response…but I suppose the answer to the question is that it's *not* pliable."

"What do you mean, *it's not pliable?*" The attendee sounded annoyed. Clearly that wasn't the answer she wanted.

"You're using Bill Gates's thinking: he has been trying

to accommodate 'legacy software'..." I gestured quote marks with my fingers, "...because almost everyone has been using the same Windows applications for years, so he thinks he's got to do it to please them. Why not say, 'Screw everybody—we're starting over'? The only reason why we're still talking about the modes and still trying to accommodate them to—or with—new technology, or theory, in this case, is because that's what we think we're *supposed* to do. I mean, who's behind it? The department chair who doesn't like change? The adjunct who's been teaching for twenty years and hasn't opened a journal, or the TA who's been thrown into the classroom with a syllabus and little else? The textbook company who wants to push its classical rhetoric in its eightieth edition because it's their number-one moneymaker? It's ridiculous, and it's futile."

A crossfire of debate that lasted a good fifteen minutes erupted between the panelists who proclaimed to have a more pliable answer to the issue of pliability, and the staunch modes supporters who attacked my attack of its credibility. I also heard hushed bickering between Macintosh loyalists and Windows traditionalists. While all this happened around me, I sank in my seat, looked down, and said nothing more. Meanwhile, Sam Vanzant sat quietly and watched the rhetorical tennis match with childlike amusement. To my relief, the facilitator announced that the session had run overtime.

As the attendees filed out, some glared at me, while others shook my hand and said they wished they'd seen my session. Maggie took advantage of the opportunity to plug our textbook. I clumsily collected my stuff—notepad, handouts, program, water bottle, shoulder bag—while participants stayed behind to bend the panelists' ears further, much to their dismay. I saw Dr. Vanzant look past them at me; in response, I raised my eyebrows at him and finally got my coat on. Just as I was about to turn to leave, he excused himself and called out to me.

"Doctor Cutrone?"

"Andrea," I replied. He extended his hand and informally introduced himself as Sam.

"I hope you're not angry with me for putting you on the spot."

"Next time, set it to *kill*, not stun."

He laughed. "Actually, I just wanted to get your attention. Besides, the Q&A was getting kind of typical, don't you think? I mean, please: the *modes*?"

His eyes were alive and round and deep blue with long lashes. Didn't he know he already had my attention?

"I remember seeing you at my session," I said.

"I was sitting in the back, behind the woman in the navy blue suit."

"They all wear navy blue suits."

"This one was kind of tall and had a mole on her neck shaped like Abe Lincoln."

I gestured with an "ah" in response, along with a laugh, and then stood for a moment of mutual grinning. I liked this guy.

"Would you like to get a drink?" he asked.

I turned to Maggie, who was standing at the doorway, wide-eyed with a toothy grin, nodding her head, then turned back to Sam.

"OK."

The hotel lounge was packed with conference attendees. Conversations about postmodern critical literary theory, community service learning, multicultural-feminist texts, electronic portfolios, wikis, blogging, and a heated argument about whether to save literature in the first-year curriculum wafted through the air, the pretension so thick it practically formed a smog. Sam, Maggie, Ron (a doctoral student from Harvard that Maggie picked up at one of the sessions), and I crammed around a table in the far corner of the lounge. I kept an eye out for Devin but soon lost myself in Sam's company. He was quite complimentary—of my presentation, my style, my appearance—and I enjoyed talking to someone other than Maggie who shared my teaching philosophy and values and humor. Like me, he was a Beatles fan and even showed *Let It Be* to his creative nonfiction classes.

While Sam went to the bar to refill my ginger ale, I went to the ladies' room. Pushing my way and leaning in towards the mirror, I powdered my nose and reapplied my lipstick. I'd dressed casually for the day's sessions: dark, boot-cut jeans; black, leather ankle boots; and a wine-colored, V-necked angora sweater that fell to the waist and flared at the sleeves. My hair had grown down to my shoulders in wispy layers. Sam said it was refreshing to see someone dressed so casually for a change.

Now what are you smiling at?

Making my way through the crowd back to the table, I bumped into several people, one of whom stopped me before I could focus.

"Cutch!"

I looked at him, startled.

Andrew.

"God, you look great," he said, eyeing me up and down.

My mouth drained of all moisture in a matter of seconds.

"Thanks."

He'd grown a beard.

"You lost weight."

I nodded.

"Diet?" he asked.

"Breast enlargement."

He switched his gaze to my chest for a few seconds, then back to my face, confused.

"So, how did your presentation go?" I asked.

"It went well. Good turnout. And yours?"

"I dropped one of my pages and made a terrific save."

"Tanya couldn't get the Power Point to work."

"I had nothing to do with it," I blurted, then felt my face turn red.

He turned an eyebrow in, and moved on in conversation. "Are you here with anyone?"

"Um, yeah. In fact, I should be getting back to him."

Thank you, God, THANK YOU, GOD, for letting me be here with a him*!!!*

Neither of us moved or spoke. Then, Andrew broke the silence.

"Married life isn't all it's cracked up to be."

What the hell is that supposed to mean?

"Yeah, well, you knew what you were getting into," I said.

"I convinced myself otherwise."

"Bullshit, Andrew," I said, enunciating each syllable of the expletive, as if they were two separate words.

"Cutch—"

"What the hell is 'Cutch'? You don't get to call me that anymore—you've lost the right to be cute and endearing with me. And you got exactly what you wanted, so don't you dare stand here and tell me you made a mistake."

"I'm not saying that."

"No? Then what are you saying?"

"Forget it," he muttered.

"You know, you haven't changed, Andrew. Still avoiding the hard questions. Still in denial about how you really feel. You lied to me. That's too bad."

"Yeah? Well, you changed too late. And *that's* too bad."

What did he mean by that? Had he made an assumption that I'd had sex with someone since him? Had my body language given away some sort of hint? Had faking it become so second nature that he actually believed something had changed? Or had something, in fact, actually changed in me?

"Maybe so." I tried to stay cool, but could feel myself becoming unnerved. I wanted a comeback, one that would leave his mouth hanging open—hell, one that would make him cry like a two-year-old. But I couldn't think of anything to say, dammit.

"Get bent, Andrew."

Without waiting for his response, I left him and went back to the ladies' room. Standing in front of the mirror yet again, I took deep breaths and dabbed my eyes with a tissue, quickly composing myself. Minutes later, I exited and walked back to my table, where Sam was waiting for me with two fresh ginger ales and a smile on his face. God, his eyes were blue.

NINETEEN

February

T HE E-MAIL EXCHANGES began the night after the Language Arts Conference ended, when Sam returned to his home in Amherst, Massachusetts. He had initiated them by asking me the questions used in the questionnaire at the end of every *Inside the Actor's Studio* episode. I responded the next morning.

```
To: samvanzant@edmund.edu
From: acutrone@brooklynu.edu
Subject: Re: the essentials
```

> Hey Sam. Here ya go.
> Q: What is your favorite word?
> A: soccer
>
> Q: What is your least favorite word?
> A: rape
>
> Q: What sound or noise do you love?
> A: The ocean.

Q: What sound or noise do you hate?
A: Balloons popping.

Q: What turns you on?
A: Junior's cheesecake

Q: What turns you off?
A: ignorance

Q: What profession would you like to attempt?
A: Cake taster

Q: What profession would you not like to attempt?
A: Flight attendant.

Q: What is your favorite curse word?
A: rat-bastard

Q: If heaven exists, what would you like to hear God say as you enter the Pearly Gates?
A: Welcome to eternity; thank you for choosing us.

Your turn.
Andi

To: acutrone@brooklynu.edu
From: samvanzant@edmund.edu
Subject: Re: the essentials

Andrea,

You asked for it...

Sam

Q: What is your favorite word?
A: batshit (runner-up: apeshit)

Q: What is your least favorite word?
A: frothy

Q: What sound or noise do you love?
A: The sound of rain hitting a windowpane.

Q: What sound or noise do you hate?
A: The sound of brakes screeching (and no,
   I didn't steal that answer from Robin
   Williams).

Q: What turns you on?
A: Right now? You. (see big smiley)

Q: What turns you off?
A: bad speling and no good grammer.

Q: What profession would you like to attempt?
A: travel writer

Q: What profession would you not like to attempt?
A: construction worker

Q: What is your favorite curse word?
A: fucknuts

Q: If heaven exists, what would you like to
   hear God say as you enter the Pearly Gates?
A: Long live Sam Vanzant!!

Later that afternoon, I called him at his office from my own, and added a question.

"What's your definition of 'hell'?" I asked.

"The Republican National Convention," he replied after a beat. "What's yours?"

I thought for a second. "Jimmy Buffet marathon."

"Ooh, that's harsh!" he said with a laugh. I could picture him holding his chest, as if he'd been shot by an arrow.

I groaned. "You're not one of *them*, are you?"

"Does that mean I've lost my chance with you?"

Unfortunately, he couldn't see the classic, electric Devin smile I was radiating.

"If the deprogramming works, you're all set."

————

More e-mails followed:

To: samvanzant@edmund.edu
From: acutrone@brooklynu.edu
Subject: NY vs. NE

Sam,

The fundamental difference between NYers and NEers are the pedestrians and drivers. In both cases, the pedestrians are equally rude, knowing they have the right of way, and they exercise this right by crossing traffic at any hour of the day and any part of the road and they expect all traffic to stop, bow down, and worship them—if they could, they'd pump their fists in the air and proclaim, "I am God." NE drivers are sissy enough to stop. But, the thing is, NY drivers are not willing to concede this right, and they will assume control by the sheer fact that they are operating a moving vehicle at 50 mph in a 35-mile zone. If the pedestrians are proclaiming their divinity, then the drivers are sure to be admitting (at the same time) that they are, in fact, the devil.

(We also have better cheesecake, but you have way better clam chowder...)
Andi

To: acutrone@brooklynu.edu
From: samvanzant@edmund.edu
Subject: Re: NY vs. NE

Andi–
You're damn right about the chowdah. I'll bet you miss the chowdah. I'll bet right now

your mouth is salivating for one spoonful. When you come to see me (when are you coming to see me, by the way?) I'm taking you to this little corner café in Amherst that has chowdah so good it'll make the Soup Nazi look like Mr. Rogers.

I find that there is very little about NY that can be considered quaint. Even those places you described in Sag Harbor, for example, don't sound authentically quaint as much as they're trying to make the cover of some magazine that sells quaintness.

Sam

P.S. So, when are you coming to see me?

.

To: samvanzant@edmund.edu
From: acutrone@brooklynu.edu
Subject: Re: NY vs. NE

Sam,
The word you're looking for is "cosmetic," or "cosmopolitan," even. And I don't even know if "quaint" is the right word. My memory of NE houses is chipping paint and stone walls. Sure, you've got your new cul-de-sacs (or is it culs-de-sac?) in Dartmouth and Taunton that are full of vinyl siding, and I noticed more and more landscapers and less ride-on mowers

from the time I left as opposed to when I first arrived. I remember how I couldn't get over all the ride-on mowers for lawns the size of my classroom. NE used to be so low maintenance—what happened?

Andi

P.S. I'm coming to see you tomorrow.

To: acutrone@brooklynu.edu
From: samvanzant@edmund.edu
Subject: Re: NY vs. NE

Andi-
The Red Sox won the World Series, that's what happened. We kicked your Yankee asses in your house and then swept the Cardinals and got drunk and knocked over telephone poles. We no longer have to feel inferior to youz guyz. We gave ourselves permission to be as hypertensive as you. Fuck quaint—we're the WORLD SERIES CHAMPIONS. That, and you guys got Bloomberg for a mayor. Or maybe it was you: your suburban high maintenance rubbed off on us.
Sam

P.S. When are you coming?

To: samvanzant@edmund.edu
From: acutrone@brooklynu.edu

Subject: Re: NY vs. NE

Two words: 26 titles.

From the cockles of my heart,

Andi

P.S. I'm coming tomorrow.

To: acutrone@brooklynu.edu
From: samvanzant@edmund.edu
Subject: Question

Dear Andi,
What do you wear to school?

To: samvanzant@edmund.edu
From: acutrone@brooklynu.edu
Subject: Answer

Dear Sam,
I swear I became a professor just so I
could wear blue jeans to work every day.
You should've seen me when I was a kid, how
I would practically fistfight my mother every time she made me wear a dress, which
was to church every Sunday, first communion,
confirmation, weddings and funerals, and the
worst, class picture days. I especially hated
picture days because I would argue that the

picture my mother would display was the one
of me from the shoulders up; but I was one
of the short kids in class so I always had
to sit in the front row and have my legs
crossed—which warranted a skirt or a dress.

But, I digress. Ah, my blue jeans: Faded.
Comfy. Sleek. Goes with any pair of shoes
I own. Everyone looks good in blue jeans,
don't you think? I'll bet you look hot in
blue jeans and a black T-shirt. I'm a sucker
for guys in blue jeans and black T-shirts…

To: acutrone@brooklynu.edu
From: samvanzant@edmund.edu
Subject: Pictureday

And I'm a sucker for Italian NY professors
who pick on current traditionalists…

What I remember about pictureday was the
combs. This was supposed to keep us occu-
pied while waiting our turn, and for boys
with ominous cowlicks, too, I guess. It was
also supposed to be a reward for not doing
anything obnoxious like crossing our eyes
at the moment of CHEEEEZE, or pushing Dennis
Kemper off his chair also at said cheese moment. But we took the combs and would slap
the girls' asses with 'em—hard. Or we'd try
to bite off the comb's teeth, or play 'em

like kazoos, or we'd use 'em for desk hockey
sticks or Chinese football goalposts. But
the cruelest use I'd ever witnessed was when
Petey Lowenstein, the biggest bully-dick of
'em all, smothered the comb in his coleslaw,
tackled said Dennis Kemper during recess,
and combed his hair with it.

Alas, now I digress. You can wear your blue
jeans any time you want. However, I would
like to see what you look like in a dress.
Preferably, a short one.

Sam

P.S. When are you coming?

To: samvanzant@edmund.edu
From: acutrone@brooklynu.edu
Subject: Re: Pictureday

Hey Sam (or should I say, Armani)-

I have a little red number that you might
like, so long as you don't make me wear it
to church…

I'm wondering if I should curse you for uncov-
ering those deliberately repressed memories
about the combs. What I remember was that the
teeth were too small for me to run through

my own hair—I saved it for my Supersized
Barbie's hair. And while we're on the subject,
if you ever snap a comb against my ass, I'll
comb your hair with melted Velveeta.

Andi, a.k.a. "The Fashionista"

P.S. Tomorrow.

———————

I was absolutely smitten with Sam.

In addition to the almost-daily e-mails, we spoke on
the phone about three times a week or sometimes text-
messaged each other, although we both hated text-message
vernacular, so by the time it took us to spell out whole
sentences, we could've called and left a voice mail or had
a quick conversation. Compared to Devin, Sam was less
shmoozy and more of a storyteller, less meticulous and
more laid back. A true memoirist, he extensively narrated
tales of growing up in Wayland, Massachusetts, with his
brother and spending a summer in Europe after college
graduation and a skiing trip in Vermont when he was
thirty where he broke his leg and hadn't been back to
the slopes since.

Sam also had no qualms about telling me how he felt
about me. His daily "when are you coming to see me"
question, either via e-mail or phone, was playful rather
than pushy. All of our conversations, both verbal and written, were pithy, fun, and flirtatious. Although wary of a

long-distance relationship, I felt a new kind of freedom, a lack of reservation or discomfort that so often accompanied me when going through the courting stage of a relationship. And despite the physical distance, we were courting. Our "dates" consisted mostly of meeting at our respective coffee shops and talking to each other on our cell phones. We tried other kinds of dates, but failed. One time we each rented the same DVD and tried to watch it at the same time while on the phone with each other, but we wound up chatting the entire time and missed the movie. An attempt to read the same Richard Russo novel also failed; our academic responsibilities quickly got in the way.

As the weeks passed and the semester kicked into gear, I found myself thinking more about Sam and less about Devin. And yet still, whenever Devin called (or, on rare occasion, we managed to get together for coffee or a movie), despite the fact that we were old friends by now, the butterflies in my stomach never really dissipated.

One day Maggie came into my office, followed by Jayce, just as I finished reading Sam's latest e-mail.

"Listen to this e-mail from Sam," I said, proceeding to read. "*I've just come out of my last class of the day and we discussed the David Sedaris essay you recommended...*' 'The Learning Curve,'" I interjected. "'*...and my students had the same reaction as yours—they couldn't get over the fact that Sedaris was encouraging his students to smoke in the classroom. Went totally batshit over it.*' Isn't that hilarious?" I said, looking up at them. "The same reaction!"

Mags and Jayce looked at each other, then at me.

"Oh my God, you're toast," Maggie said.

"What are you talking about?"

"You're in love with this guy!"

"I'm smitten with him."

"Oh, pardon me—you're *smitten* with him. Are you listening to yourself? So when's the wedding?"

"Will you stop?" I said, annoyed.

"Does Devin know?" Jayce asked.

"Know what?"

"That you're long-distance-dating Sam."

"Not exactly," I said sheepishly.

"You're kidding," Maggie said. "It's been what— five, six weeks? You haven't said a word to him all this time?"

"It's not like Devin and I have been seeing a helluva lot of each other these days, if at all. And we only talk on the phone once a week now, sometimes less."

"Why? What happened?" Jayce asked.

"Nothing, really. He was swamped with dates during the holidays, but since then, I don't know."

"Maybe you both just got used to not hanging out with each other," said Jayce.

"Maybe he got himself a girlfriend!" said Maggie. The thought had never crossed my mind, yet my gut tightened and Mags, observant best friend that she is, noticed.

"Why should that bother you if you're seeing Sam?"

"Who said it bothers me? It's not like Devin and I were ever dating. And who says I'm 'seeing' Sam?"

"Devin's the guy you sleep with. Sam's the guy you have breakfast with," Maggie said.

I looked at her, perplexed. "What does that mean?"

"Maybe she's in love with both of them," Jayce said to Maggie, as if I weren't there.

"I am not in love with two men!" I said staunchly.

"Come on, Andi! There's nothing wrong with it," said Jayce.

"Have you ever been in love with two men at the same time? And I don't mean your boyfriend and Taye Diggs."

Jayce smirked. "Honey, I got over both of them a long time ago. And while it's never happened to me personally, I still think it's totally possible."

"What about you, Mags? Ever been in love with two men at the same time?"

She contemplated this.

"It depends on the men, I guess."

Jayce and I exchanged confused glances.

"Does Sam know about Devin?" Jayce asked.

"Look, I am not in love with two men," I said again, perhaps too emphatically, circumventing Jayce's question. "And as far as Sam is concerned, well, it just is what it is. It's…fun. Actually, it's what everyone says being with Devin the Escort is supposed to be like. There's no pressure to it. Better yet, I don't have to shell out my life savings or sign a bogus contract for a couple of hours with him."

"Suit yourself," Maggie said. "But the sooner you come clean with yourself and everyone else, the better off you'll be."

I knew she was right, even though I didn't give her the satisfaction of telling her so. And I knew it was long overdue.

TWENTY

March

DEVIN CALLED one Saturday afternoon, and in separate cars we drove out to Claudio's in Greenport for dinner.

"So what's up?" I spoke after we were seated and opened our menus. "I haven't seen you in ages. And what were you doing on the Island today?"

"I had a get-together with my family," he said, looking at his menu in an evasive manner.

"Special occasion?"

"My mother's birthday."

"How was it?" I asked, knowing Devin's relationship with his family was strained, at best. He never talked much about it, though.

"It was fine." His terse response indicated that he wanted to continue that trend.

I perused my menu and settled on the shrimp scampi. He ordered the swordfish. Once the menus were out of our hands, we looked at each other awkwardly, as if on a first date, and a blind one at that.

"So . . ." I started. He raised his eyebrows, indicating for me to continue, but I couldn't think of anything to say.

"How's work?" he asked.

"You mean school?" It rarely felt like work to me in the laborious sense. "It's fine."

"Good classes?"

"Yeah. The usual, I guess. Not bad. How 'bout you?"

"The usual," he responded, without following up. Neither of us seemed to want to talk about Devin's work anymore.

"I've got spring break next week," I said.

"Any plans?"

"Maggie and I are driving down to Florida for a few days. I know that's a bit clichéd, Florida and spring break. Then I'm going up to Massachusetts for the weekend."

His eyes widened. "Really?"

"Yeah, it's been a while since I've been back. I'm looking forward to it, actually."

"Are you going to visit anyone in particular?"

I swore in that moment he knew. Had Maggie said something to him? Or did he think I meant Andrew? I had told him about running into Andrew at the conference. *Tell him! TELL HIM!!*

"Just some friends," I said.

Nice telling.

"Well, have a good time, I guess," he said with all the enthusiasm of someone about to take a final exam.

"I will," I said.

We spent much of dinner making the same kind of small talk, and I wondered how we'd become so shallow, wistful for the days when hours passed like minutes, our conversations a never-ending wellspring. I missed the private jokes we'd accumulated. I missed our laughing. I missed those times when silence didn't feel so forced.

It was almost as if there were a glass partition separating the two of us, like at a prison.

As I drove back to East Meadow, all I could think about was how much I couldn't wait to see Sam.

———————

Maggie and I fought like sisters in the car throughout most of the drive down to Orlando. Once there, I spent the next three days on the beach preoccupied with and anticipating the fast-approaching weekend. In addition to seeing Sam, I'd also scheduled a second interview and teaching demonstration at Northampton University on Friday, upon their request. Maggie was still in the dark regarding the job prospect, and I felt guilty about not telling her, which was probably why I was picking fights to begin with.

On Wednesday and Thursday, I rode the Amtrak to Boston, where Sam met me at South Station, a bouquet of flowers in his hand. To my surprise, we both practically ran on the platform to reach each other; had our hands not been full, I'll bet he would've picked me up and spun me around when we finally embraced. He kissed me full on the lips—it was heavenly. It had taken Devin four months just to kiss me on the cheek. It took Sam less than four seconds from the time I got off the train.

If I didn't know any better, I'd swear I'd just come home.

Northampton University put me up in a nearby Comfort Inn. After a late dinner, Sam dropped me off at the hotel and kissed me good night. Soft and subtle and perfect.

The interview at NU the next day was an all-day affair. Mentally spent and physically exhausted from the traveling, I called Sam and then spent the night by myself, crashed out in my hotel room. He picked me up for breakfast at a little nook the following morning. We spent the day walking through the main part of town in Amherst. He also took me to Edmund College and gave me a tour. We then picnicked next to the lake on its campus. The weather was sunny, yet brisk—typical for New England in March. Sam was quite affectionate and polite, holding doors open and making sure I was comfortable. He even *asked permission* to hold my hand. Never had I experienced such chivalry, even from Devin with all his charm. I'd never noticed it before, but Devin seemed to always have an agenda, as if he were always three moves ahead of you, like a chess player. Sam was much more in the moment.

And so was I. My typical preoccupation with what I was wearing or how my hair looked was nonexistent, especially since the NU interview ended. In fact, in terms of makeup, I wore little other than cherry-flavored lip-gloss all weekend.

Just as I finished munching on biscotti, I found Sam gazing intently at me, expressing a soft smile.

"May I kiss you?" he asked.

I nodded without hesitation, and he leaned in and planted a sensational kiss on my lips. If the power were to go out in one of Edmund College's buildings, the fuse could be recharged by sticking our fingers in a socket following that kiss.

After the picnic and a matinee, we sat in Sam's favorite coffee shop, gawking at each other like college kids and wearing mischievous grins.

"Wanna see my house?" he asked.

"Sure!" I replied, and we jumped up as if in a mad race to the car.

Sam's house was a twentieth-century colonial with weathered wood shingles and fading painted shutters. Inside, hardwood floors and low ceilings added to the New England coziness that I had forgotten about but now enveloped me. Mismatched, dark leather furniture resided in every room, along with bookcases filled to capacity and the pleasant smell of burning hickory. Despite the draft leaking through the old wood windows, the house exuded utter warmth.

We sat on the floor in the living room, in front of the unlit fireplace, Steely Dan barely audible on the stereo.

"Want me to get a fire going?" he asked.

"Seems like there already is one," I replied. My boldness surprised me; it felt natural in the moment.

This time, he skipped the request for permission, and kissed me hard. I actually fell over, inches away from the edge of the couch and a concussion. We giggled and moved out of harm's way and made out. I felt free, light, uninhibited. *This is it*, I thought. *I'm ready. This is what I want, and who I want it with.*

"Wanna go to bed?" I asked between kisses.

Wow! Did that really come out of my mouth? A twinge of doubt crept in. I could hear Devin's voice coaching me, *just relax...*

"I mean..." I sat up. "I don't wanna be too forward."

Good grief. Can I hit my head now?

Sam sat up and looked at me warmly.

"Forward is good," he said, and kissed my neck. I let out a soft moan; it'd been a while.

"I like that," I whispered, my breathing getting heavy.

"I like *you*," he cooed.

"What else do you like?" I asked, taking his hand and slipping it under my blouse.

It was Sam's turn to stop. He took his hand away and propped himself against the couch. For a split second he looked like he wanted to hit his head, too.

"Are you OK? Did I do something wrong?"

He looked at me as if the notion was absurd. "Of course not."

"Then, what is it?"

"Andrea," he started. I loved the way he always used my full name—there was something sexy about the way he said it. "Sweetheart, there's nothing I want more than to make love to you right here and right now."

Uh-oh. I felt a big "but" coming on.

"But I don't wanna just screw you and send you on your way, as if that's all this weekend was about."

"I never thought that was your intention." I paused for a beat and looked at him. "What *is* this weekend about?"

He took my hand into his. "Over the course of these past couple of months, I think I've fallen in love with you. In fact, I *know* it."

A look of bewilderment overtook me, as if no man had ever told me he loved me before. And I suddenly realized it was because I'd never really *believed* any one of them who did. My subconscious simply wouldn't allow it. But thanks to meeting Devin, that had changed. And seeing the look in Sam's ocean blue eyes, not only did I believe him, but I also *knew*. And yet, I couldn't bring myself to say I loved him too, although I was pretty sure I did.

Without waiting for my response, he took my other hand into his as well, cradling them both.

"If I'm moving too fast, just tell me and I'll back off. But I want this to be something serious, and I don't want us to have sex until we *both* want it to be, OK?"

Was this really happening?

"You're saying you don't want to sleep with me tonight?" I had to make sure I was hearing him correctly.

"No, I totally want to sleep with you tonight! I mean, I want you to spend the night and I want us to cuddle in bed and stuff."

The "and stuff" intrigued me.

"But having sex and then going back to this long-distance thing just doesn't seem right or fair to either one of us, don't you agree?"

The fucking irony!

After what seemed like eons of dead air, I burst out laughing, one of those laughs that indicates you're one step away from mania.

"What's so funny?" he asked.

"Man, wait till I tell you. Talk about fucknuts…" I said, laughing again. Sam waited for me to calm down. "Seriously, though. I do agree with you." I stifled a chuckle. *What does "and stuff" consist of?* I wanted to ask.

"Look, I don't wanna be pushy and I don't wanna scare you off, but I really hope you get that position at NU. And if you don't, then I hope you move back here anyway. Otherwise, hell, I'll just move to New York."

"You would really do that?"

"Yes, I would."

"Give up your tenure and everything?"

"In a New York minute, as they say."

"Wow," I said, my heart fluttering lightly.

"Yeah."

"The Yankees fans'll kill you. After they eat you for breakfast, of course."

He laughed softly and kissed me playfully on my nose before holding me close. Everything about Sam felt good to me.

He'd actually relocate for me! Quit his job, leave tenure, and everything! No one had ever made such a sincere gesture before. Hell, even if they had, it would've scared the crap out of me, and vice versa if I had made such an offer. I thought about what he said about my moving back to Massachusetts even if the job at NU didn't work out. Was I willing to take that risk? I further thought about what Jayce said about my being in love with two men. Saying yes to a serious relationship with Sam was saying no to the false hope that one day things would actually change with Devin. And wasn't that worth letting go? Was I ready to do so?

I stood up. "Got a T-shirt or something for me to sleep in?"

He leapt up like a kid on Christmas Eve who'd just been bribed to bed by the promise of presents come morning. Soon after, we snuggled under a navy blue comforter. Sam smelled like a combination of Ivory soap and patchouli oil. I breathed in the scent and breathed out a sigh.

"What's that for?" he practically whispered, spooning me.

"This is nice," I said.

He let out his own sigh.

"What's *that* for?" I asked in mock imitation.

"There's a beautiful woman next to me in my bed."

Oh, sweet mother of pearl. Like buttuh.

Just as I was drifting off, he asked, "So what were you laughing at before?"

And as plainly as he asked the question, I plainly answered him. I told him everything, about growing up and my father and brothers and my sexual inhibitions and my current sexual status. He listened intently, asking me a question or two along the way, stroking my hair while he held me. For the first time, I harbored no anxiety or shame, no fear of rejection or judgment. And I received none. In fact, he held me even closer. "That is the coolest thing I've ever heard," he said. "Makes me feel even better about not going all the way tonight."

"I would've, though," I said. "I'm ready for it. And willing."

"Not yet. When you move here, then you'll be ready. Note that I said 'when.'"

"Noted," I replied, my voice growing faint.

The only part I left out was Devin and our arrangement. OK, so maybe I harbored just a little bit of fear. All I said was that I had learned a lot in the past year and gained a lot of confidence. A reinterpreted truth.

I sighed again.

What seemed like a long time but was perhaps no more than five minutes passed.

"I hope I get the NU gig, too," I said.

Eventually, I fell asleep to the rhythm of his breathing.

TWENTY-ONE

THE NEXT MORNING, Sam and I awoke at almost the same time, and we fooled around for a bit before he got up to find an extra toothbrush for me and cook us breakfast. (I learned what "and stuff" was.) Feeling a chill, I put on his flannel robe and went to the bathroom to freshen up, not feeling the slightest bit of apprehension regarding my morning breath or scraggly hair.

As I descended the creaky stairs, the smell of sizzling bacon and fresh-brewed coffee intensified. Sam stood in front of the stove, dressed in flannel pajama pants, ratty socks, a heather-gray Edmund College hoodie, and glasses, flipping one pancake and peeking under another. You'd think he was dressed in Armani, the way I checked him out. He seemed to be thinking the same thing about me when he saw me shuffle in.

"Hey, gorgeous!"

I looked over my shoulder to see if there was someone else behind me. He laughed. "You are so funny, Andrea."

"Smells yummy in here," I said as I walked to where he was standing and gave him a kiss.

"Bacon and coffee are the two best smells in the world."

I begged to differ. "Hardly."

"What, then?"

"Freshly baked anything is the best smell."

"What's the worst?"

"Dead skunk."

He conceded.

He set the feast on an enormous butcher-block table: bacon, sausage, pancakes and Vermont maple syrup, coffee, orange juice, and scrambled eggs.

"Holy cow!" I exclaimed as he started loading my plate. "Has my Italian grandmother taken over your body? Are you trying to give me a coronary?"

"Breakfast is the best meal of the day and you know it!"

"I like to save room for lunch and dinner, too!"

"Well, why not take a cue from the Italians and indulge in our pleasures—good food and good company."

"*Buon appetito*," I said.

As I slowly savored every enjoyable bite, I couldn't help but think of what Maggie said about Sam being the guy you have breakfast with. A sense of satisfaction filled me, and it wasn't just from the comfort food.

After we did the dishes, he put his arms around me. "So, what shall we do today before I so reluctantly send you back to Long Island?"

A devious look crossed my face as several ideas came to mind.

We held and kissed each other on the platform at South Station for a long time before we finally let go and I stepped onto the Amtrak train bound for New York. Finding it hard to concentrate on the book I'd brought to pass the time, I leaned back and relaxed in my seat, closed my eyes, and happily replayed the weekend's events in my mind until I fell asleep to the rhythm of the train's swaying and bumps across the tracks. I didn't turn my cell phone on until I got back to the city that night, where I decided to stay at Maggie's since it was so late and school resumed the next day. I called Sam to let him know I'd made it home safely. Then I listened to a message from Devin: "Hey, Andi, it's me. I was just wondering if you got back yet. Give me a call."

Maggie grilled me about the weekend, as I'd expected her to.

"You slept with him, didn't you. I can see it on your face. So how was it?"

"Well...yes and no. Would you believe he wanted to wait?"

Her jaw dropped. "Are you kidding me? *He* did?"

I nodded my head methodically and made a "scout's honor" gesture with my fingers.

"Why?" she asked in disbelief.

"Said he didn't wanna screw me and send me off. Said he wanted us to commit to something serious before having sex. And believe me, I was all set to go. I mean, I would've done it if he changed his mind."

"Wow," she said, stunned. "I didn't think there were still guys in the world like that."

"Apparently they've all left New York."

"So you didn't do anything all weekend?"

"I didn't say that," I said, giving her a Devin-style wink.

Maggie picked up a pillow from the couch and threw it at me. "You little tease!"

I caught the pillow and threw it back at her. "What can I say? I don't kiss and tell!"

"So? Is it serious? I mean, what's going to happen?"

"I don't know yet," I said, my voice trailing off.

"When are you gonna tell Devin?"

"When there's something to tell him, I guess."

"I think there already is. After all, I'm guessing you used some of his moves this weekend."

"His instruction came in handy, yes." I paused as a thought came to me. "Do you think he had an opportunity to do some writing this weekend?"

We both took a second to ponder this, then burst into laughter. The next day, when I came back to East Meadow after school, two more messages from Devin awaited me on my landline:

"Hey, are you there? Did you get lost in the wilderness somewhere? Give me a call…"

"Hey, Andi. It's Devin…um, I guess you're not back from your visit yet. I was hoping we could catch a movie or something. It's been a while since we've done that. Anyway, give me a call when you get this message. "

I didn't call him back for another day.

A month passed. By the end of April, Northampton University called to offer me the position.

TWENTY-TWO

May

W HY?" MAGGIE CRIED in her office when I broke
the news about my leaving.

"It's a good opportunity. Writing program director,
better salary, tenure track…"

"No, I mean, why didn't you tell me you were thinking
of leaving?"

"Because I didn't want you to talk me out of it."

"You're damn right I would've talked you out of it.
I'm going to talk you out of it now." She put her head in
her hands and sighed. "The textbook is coming out just
in time for the College Writing Conference in Hartford."

"So, we'll cover more ground if you're plugging it there
and I'm plugging it in Northampton."

"Are you moving because of Sam?"

"I had the interview before I met Sam."

"Devin?"

I didn't answer.

"You're running away," she said, shaking and pointing her finger at me, parental-like. I sucked in a breath.

"No, I'm not. I came here because I was running away
from Andrew. I've been gallivanting around Manhattan
all these months, but it isn't where I belong."

"But you still love the Island. I know you do. Go to Dowling or Suffolk Community or SUNY Stony Brook. They're all hiring"

"Mags, I miss Massachusetts."

"Since when?"

"I don't know. For a while now, I guess. Seeing Sam brought it all back."

"You'll never get a decent bagel ever again."

"I'll survive. I did before."

"Oh, fuck it," she said in defeat. "It's a directorship. You're ready for it. It's just that this place has been so much *fun* since you came. Who's going to come into my office and read me papers and talk theory and tell stories?"

That did it. We both sat and cried. Maybe Mags was right. Maybe I was running away from Devin. Or maybe I was running to Sam.

Devin and I hardly ever saw or spoke to each other anymore. I rationalized that some cosmic force was responsible, easing the painful process of separation. Could it be construed as breaking up? I wondered. We were never dating. And yet, we'd spent hours engaged in stimulation—both intellectual and sexual. We exchanged fluids of meaningful conversation; quiet, intimate moments; knowing glances; and occasional bouts of heavy breathing. We saw each other completely naked—metaphorically, that is—and tapped into all our possibilities in the midst of our flaws. Together, we practiced the craft of revision.

"Have you still not told Devin about Sam?" Maggie asked.

"I haven't really had the chance."

Maggie gave me a look of skepticism.

"Why should I tell him anything?"

"Because that might change things for him. He might admit that he has feelings for you."

"Forget it, Mags. If he hasn't said anything by now, he never will."

"Does Sam know about Devin?"

I gave her a look that said, *Stop grilling me.*

"I like Sam," she said, as if casting her vote. "He's so cute. And he's obviously into you. Then again, Devin's just so..."

"I know," I said, reading her mind, feeling that flutter I always felt when I thought of him.

How was I going to tell him I was leaving? How was I going to walk away from him? Did I even want to?

———

At our usual diner, my mother and I sat opposite one another in the booth, her jacket draped over her bare shoulders, as usual.

"Sooo, Mom. I have some news."

"You're seeing someone?"

I frowned, already exasperated with her. "No—well, yeah, but that's not the news. I got a faculty and writing program administrator position at Northampton University in Massachusetts. Professor status, tenure track, good salary. I'm moving next month."

She put her fork down onto her plate and looked at me, stunned.

"You just left there."

"I've been here for two years, Mom."

"Oh, excuse me. I didn't realize that's a lifetime."

"What's the big deal?"

"All this floating around doesn't look good on a re-sume, Andi."

"Who's 'floating'? I spent three years getting my PhD, a year as part-timer, and two years in a full-time, non-tenure-track teaching and administrative position. I've also pub-lished three articles, delivered papers at conferences every year since grad school, and cowrote a textbook that's com-ing out any day now. So tell me where 'floating' comes in."

She remained unimpressed. "Have you told your broth-ers yet?"

"I called them last night."

"They're going on the road again, I think, so I don't know if they'll be able to help you with the move."

"I'll have it covered," I said, thinking of either tapping Devin or Sam—a thought of the two of them showing up and having a duel over me crossed my mind.

She picked up her fork again and poked it into her salad.

"What's this about your seeing someone?"

"His name is Sam, and he's also a writing professor."

"At Brooklyn U?"

"No, he's in Massachusetts, not far from where I'll be, actually."

"So, you're leaving for a man?"

I huffed. "Give me a little credit, Mom. I'm leaving for the *job*. Sam happened to be a pleasant surprise, a coincidence."

"How long have you known him?"

"Since January."

"You've been long-distance dating him?"

"Pretty much."

She paused. "Well, I guess it's bon voyage, then. As long as you're happy."

"I am. Aren't *you* happy for me?"

"Sure. I guess it's back to the Cross Sound Ferry for me."

"Just remember your sunscreen," I said, deflated.

And that was that. No tearful breakdown, like Maggie. Then again, she'd never cried when I'd left the first time, nor when my brothers left. Maybe she cried when we weren't around. But I would've preferred to see some display of affection. I needed to know that she cared, that I wasn't just some acquaintance passing through her life. Hell, just once I wanted her to be *proud* of me. But I had learned to stop waiting for things that never happen.

Mags, Mom, my brothers...all done. And of course, Sam knew—he was the first person I told. He yeeee-hawwed like a cowboy.

That left one more person.

———

After two weeks of phone tagging, Devin and I finally touched base and arranged to meet at Junior's one late Tuesday afternoon. As it turned out, we sat at the same booth as the first time we'd gotten together, the day I'd proposed the arrangement. It simultaneously felt like yesterday and a lifetime ago. Our long conversations had been reduced to one-syllable small talk. Every utterance was a strain; you'd think there was an actual wall between us, and we were exerting all our strength to remove it.

"You're unusually quiet," he remarked.

The moment had arrived, and I knew it. And in that instant, all fear vanished.

I paused before responding. Tears filled my eyes as I took his hand.

"I think you're my best friend," I said. The realization of the words astonished me.

I paused again.

"I love you, Dev. And I'm leaving."

His hand still in mine, he sat frozen for a few seconds; then he blinked and shook his head slightly.

"What did you say?"

"I accepted a teaching position at Northampton University. I'm moving back to Massachusetts."

"When?"

"Next month, after the semester ends."

"When did this happen?"

"I interviewed back in January."

"Why didn't you tell me?"

"I didn't tell anyone. Not even Maggie."

He looked past me at nothing, bewildered. Then he darted his eyes back to mine. "Did you also say you love me?" he asked.

"Yes."

My voice was shaking; my heart, pounding.

"As in, you're in love with me?"

"Yes."

"Since when?"

"Since the day we met. I just didn't admit it to myself until that night of the final."

He looked into his coffee cup, slowly and silently. "I don't know what to say," he barely whispered.

"I'm sorry. I didn't mean to drop both bombs like this. They just sort of fell out of my mouth at the same time."

"Why didn't you tell me sooner?"

"That I was in love with you? Because you forbade it, remember? We signed that fucking contract. And then, when the contract expired, I didn't think there was any chance of it working out. I mean, you were right, Dev. I could never fully approve of what you do for a living. And that's totally hypocritical of me to say, considering I used you. You were right about that, too. I was no different from any of your clients."

"I was way out of line when I said that," he said.

"But you weren't wrong. We used each other."

"To better ourselves. We both benefited from it. You taught me a lot, Andi."

"And you taught me a lot, and I am so grateful to you for that."

"But why do you have to leave?"

"I'm ready for more. And less, too, I suppose. I'm ready for a more challenging position as both a writing program director and a published textbook author. I wanna publish a collection of memoirs next. And I'm ready for a more fulfilling, stable relationship, too. I met someone at the conference back in January."

He stiffened. "Really."

"His name is Sam. He teaches at Edmund College, and we've been e-mailing and calling each other. In fact, he's the person I went to see during spring break. We're going to start seeing each other seriously once I move. I think I'm—I really, really care about him a lot. And you know, that's something else that's changed since meeting you. I never got to really *know* a man before. I was always so preoccupied with the sex thing and whether I was satisfying him and terrified of being rejected. By spending all this time with you, I got to know you. And I got to know and be myself—my real self. I just sometimes wish we could've started it this way and not as a proposition. And yet, in its own way, it's the most honest relationship I've ever been in, I think. And I guess now I wanna try that with someone else."

I paused, but not long enough to let him speak before sheepishly adding, "I should've told you sooner, I know. I'm sorry about that. I don't know why I didn't."

He looked straight into my eyes, fully absorbing everything, as always.

"And the less?" he said meekly. "You said you were ready for more and less."

"For as long as I can remember, I wanted to live the life of a single New Yorker. I wanted to be a part of the city, part of a scene—coffee shops, bookstores, galleries, dating, whatever; knowing my way around, riding the subway fearlessly... All those years in New England, I passed myself off as that New Yorker. But I never was. I faked it. I was just a sheltered girl from the Long Island suburbs. This past year, I lived the life I always wanted, and you know what? I was still faking it. I was trying to cover up so much: my body, my sexuality, my insecurity, my fear...

"But not anymore. I'm still a suburban girl at heart; I'm just not a sheltered, frightened girl anymore. Strange, I'm neither a New Yorker nor a New Englander. Or maybe I'm both now. I don't know. But I don't need the city streets and the train and the noise anymore. I don't need the crowds or the skyscrapers or Junior's or Heartland. I don't need to take cover."

Devin drew in a breath. "Well, sounds like you've made up your mind."

"What about *you*, Dev?"

"What about me?"

"Aren't you ready for more? You once told me that I'm more than my body. So are you. *You can do so much more.* Don't you want more...and less?"

A deep sadness overshadowed the color of his eyes from sienna to charcoal gray.

"Why don't you go all the way with your clients?" I asked.

The question loomed in the air as he looked away, eyes dark, searching for words. Then his eyes met mine earnestly.

Before he could answer me, his cell phone rang. He took the call when he saw the number, spoke abruptly, and ended with, "I'll be right there." He looked alarmed.

"Is everything OK?"

"I gotta go." He got up, grabbed his coat, and headed for the door while I jumped up to follow him.

"What happened?"

He turned to me. "It's my father."

He then ran out the door without saying good-bye.

TWENTY-THREE

I DIDN'T HEAR from Devin for a week, and he didn't return my calls. What's more, he wasn't at his apartment when I went there and spoke to the doorman, who knew me well by now. When I tracked down Christian, Devin's business partner, he told me that Devin had canceled all his clients' dates indefinitely.

"Why?" I asked. "What happened?"

"You know I can't discuss it with you. You're a client."

"Past tense, Christian. The contract expired a long time ago. We're friends now."

"Which I've never understood—Devin's never gotten personal with any of his clients, past or present. Besides, if you two are such good friends, then how come he hasn't told you himself?"

Good question.

"Seems to me like he doesn't want you to know," he said.

I huffed in exasperation.

"Christian, please. I know you're cautious and distrusting of my intentions, and you have every right to be, given the nature of your business. But you also know I was never your typical client."

Silence.

"Look, he's your *friend,* isn't he?"

Christian paused. "Yes, he is."

"Well, he's my friend too. Sometimes our friends don't ask for support when they need it. I think Devin needs me. What do you think?"

Although the silence lasted only a second or two, in that eternity I felt my heart sink in defeat. Just as I was ready to hang up the phone, Christian spoke.

"His father died. The funeral is tomorrow. I don't know where, though."

"Thank you, Christian." I pushed the words past the lump in my throat, and then I hung up.

Despite the relief of knowing, my insides swirled with sickness; I had sensed this truth all along.

TWENTY-FOUR

THROUGHOUT THE TIME that Devin and I spent together, he'd rarely mentioned his family. What I knew about his father I had learned through his writing:

> He was a former construction worker who had to quit at the age of thirty because of an accident on the job. The injury resulted in a lifetime of chronic back pain and disability checks. He went back to school and got an associate's degree in accounting, and kept the books for several construction companies, while Mom worked in the town school district as an administrative assistant. Dad was a gruff, burly man who preferred beer and boxing to Bach and Botticelli. He read little outside of Car and Driver, the sports section of Newsday, and an occasional trade magazine, although he always loved World War II stories...

He saw Devin's passions for art and music and film as "fag stuff." He was resentful when Devin was accepted to Parsons, and could only afford SUNY Binghamton. He was disappointed when Devin majored in art history.

("You'll be lucky if you get a job as a goddamn tour guide," his father once said. Then Devin told him that docents don't even get paid...) To placate him, Devin changed his major to business and picked up a minor in art history. And when he moved into the city and eventually started the escort business with Christian, his father practically stopped speaking to him altogether, unimpressed with his son's knack for business and promotion and selling.

"I tried to raise you to be a man with self-respect and decency," his father had once told him. *"I'd rather see you cleaning toilets than being some sissy-boy who wears nice suits and goes to fancy restaurants with some broad who's too stupid or ugly to get it for free."*

Thing is, Devin's father never respected him. And I couldn't help but wonder if Devin became an escort in an attempt to prove to his father that he *was* a man.

His eyes widened when he saw me coming up the church steps, just before the service.

"What are you doing here?" he asked.

"I had to drag it out of Christian, the rat-bastard."

"How'd you know where to come?"

"I looked in the obits under 'Santino' and remembered you telling me that you were from Massapequa."

He looked at me, his eyes filled with remorse.

"I'm sorry I never called you back," he said.

I gave him a smile of reassurance, and then hugged him. "You had more important things to do."

He squeezed me and took a deep breath.

"I'm so sorry for your loss, Dev," I whispered in his ear, squeezing him back. He reluctantly let go.

I didn't sit with him during the funeral mass, but we made eye contact a few times, and I affectionately smiled at him, feeling a strange kind of warmth, more like something one would feel at a wedding than a funeral. I'd never seen this side of him. He looked so reserved on the outside, dressed not in his usual Versace but black slacks, a finely woven, white button-down shirt without a tie, and the Helmut Lang sport jacket he wore when he showed up at Heartland with Della Mason. Not the charmer, the crowd-worker, the man who always knew how to make a woman feel special and safe. Rather, he looked as if the wheels were spinning in his head, fighting to keep composure. He looked *vulnerable.*

After the funeral, he invited me to his parents' house and rode with me in my car. We were silent during most of the drive. As we got off Sunrise Highway, he spoke.

"It was cancer."

I had suspected that. I kept my eyes on the road, following the procession of limos.

"When did it start?"

"A year ago. They told him he had six months."

"Where was it?"

"It started in his pancreas but spread to his lungs. He was a two-pack-a-day smoker before he quit fifteen years ago."

"Did you know he had cancer?"

"My mother told me when he was first diagnosed. He's been bad these last couple of months—in and out of the hospital—that's why I wasn't around much. When I got the call at Junior's, he was at the end. He died two days later."

"Did you get to say good-bye?"

He didn't answer me. We pulled into a long, narrow driveway leading up to a tan, colonial house.

Inside the house, Devin introduced me to his family; his mother and two sisters greeted me warmly. I expected judgment from them, expected them to wonder, *Is she one of "them"?* The living room and kitchen were crowded with relatives and friends of Devin's father. I looked at family photographs on and above the mantle: Disney World in '82—barely smiling. High school graduation in '86—hair moussed and layered and practically down to his shoulders, those same sienna eyes sparkling. I'll bet every girl had a crush on him. Next, his sister's wedding photo, all of them standing in a row, distinguished, with Devin standing next to his father—then healthy and proud and commanding—both dressed in tuxes. They looked alike, albeit his father was a bit more rough around the edges.

I studied the photos, and slowly the revelation came into focus: none of them was of Devin. I was really looking at *David*, who, despite his model looks and popularity, lived in lonely solitude and needed to be loved by his father.

This wasn't the man I'd spent the last year with. This wasn't the man I knew.

And then, it became stunningly clear to me, when I saw him standing across the room, talking to his Uncle Larry, shy, almost awkward, plain: *he's been faking it all this time.* Then, I saw him—*really* saw him. Not on paper. Not in a bathtub. Then, I knew. And in that moment, I felt very out of place in this house, with this family. I felt like a stranger, an intruder, a voyeur.

"So, how did you and David meet?" Devin's sister Joannie asked me as I helped wrap up and put away leftovers. I froze: I wasn't used to hearing him referred to as "David" and had been consciously making an effort all day to not call him "Devin" and be found out. Perhaps they were, in fact, wondering whether I was a client (an escort for the escort, I thought; how ironic). My mind raced for an answer that wasn't a lie, but rather a reinterpretation of the truth.

"We met at a cocktail party and became friends soon thereafter," I replied, my voice shaking a bit. I was sure they were convinced I was lying—and wasn't sure they were wrong to think so.

"And what do you do?"

"I'm a professor and an assistant director of college writing at Brooklyn U."

Joannie probably knew nothing about Devin's business, and assumed, as I once had, that a professor wouldn't seek out an escort's service. She leaned in a bit and spoke in a low, hushed voice.

"You know what my brother does for a living?"

"Yes, I do."

"And you're *OK* with it?" she asked, appalled.

My insides tightened. "Well, I think I'd be less tolerant of it if we were dating, but otherwise, it's his choice."

That sounded plausible.

"Makes me sick," she said, her voice now turning somewhat venomous. "Someone so talented, cheapening himself. Did you know that he had a scholarship to Parsons? Have you ever seen his paintings?"

I didn't know that. And then it dawned on me that some of the paintings in his apartment, the ones signed *Santino*, were his. Why had I never made the connection? Why had he never told me?

I felt the need to defend him. "I thought he couldn't afford Parsons," I said.

Joannie's sister Rosalyn joined the conversation. "Our father wasn't too keen on him going to art school, or being in the city. He was always afraid David would be gay as a result. He wasn't exactly a modern thinker in that regard."

"But prostituting himself? Dad was less than keen on that, too," Joannie rebuked.

"Still, you gotta give him credit for building a successful business from the ground up," I said, my voice still mousy and nervous. "And, from what I know—from what he tells me, he's good at what he does. I mean, his clients appreciate him."

This neither impressed nor persuaded her.

"But there's got to be something else he can do. Something we can be proud of, and not so scandalous and sordid."

"There's always something else we can do," I said, "if only we weren't so busy listening to other people's voices."

Joannie didn't respond. Perhaps she was just as confused by the comment as I was. Or perhaps it was because Devin came into the kitchen.

I walked back into the living room. As I looked around the room at the remaining family members scattered about, I saw a little girl sprawled on the carpet in the far corner of the room, coloring pictures, seemingly invisible to everyone else. Had she been there all this time? I wondered. I walked over and knelt down beside her, my long, A-line skirt fanning out and covering some of the finished drawings.

"Whatcha drawin'?"

She looked up at me, wary of the stranger looming over her. Without speaking, she showed me a crayon meadow of wildflowers.

"Mmmmm…pretty."

She looked at me quizzically.

"What's your name?" she asked.

"Andi."

She frowned. "That's a *boy's* name."

I smiled and let out a little laugh. "It can be a girl's name, too. Actually, it's a nickname. My real name is Andrea. What's your name?"

"Meredith."

"Do your mom and dad call you Merry?"

"They call me Missy."

"Ah. So you have a nickname just like I do."

"My grandpa's dead."

She stabbed me with her bluntness, yet also touched me with her honesty.

"I know." I paused anxiously, searching for something meaningful to say in response. "Does that make you sad?"

"A little," she said. She showed me another drawing of stick figures and a square house with a triangle roof. "Maybe I'll see him again next year." She had flaxen hair down to the middle of her back that curled at the ends. She then added, "I'm gonna be six."

I wanted to cry.

I asked Meredith if I could color with her, and then became completely engrossed with her and covered the carpet with drawings of flowers and puppies and stick figures; we shared crayons and signed our names to each work of art. She signed one of mine for me, spelling A-N-D-Y.

"Hey, you've got enough for an exhibit!" The sound of Devin's voice from behind rattled me and caused me to flinch like I do when a balloon pops. I whisked around and looked up so quickly that my neck cricked. He towered over me.

"Geez, you scared me!" I said. "How long you been there?"

"Not long," he replied. He was looking at me almost the same way we'd looked at each other in the MOMA that day, when we were talking about Maggie's and my book. He looked at me the way Sam did.

———

Late afternoon had quickly faded into evening, which then morphed into night. I insisted that Devin stay with me at my apartment rather than at the house. He took me up on the offer. His family welcomed me back to the house anytime.

We were quiet in the car.

"I know you're probably sick of everyone asking this, but are you OK?" I asked.

"Yeah, I'm fine. Thanks for being here today, and letting me stay with you."

"No problem. Can you imagine you going all the way back into the city and getting caught in the traffic?"

"No, I mean it." He reached out and touched my arm. "You don't know how it felt to see your face today. And I could never stay in that house tonight, or go back into the city. You don't know how much it means to me that you even knew to come."

"What do you mean, that I *knew* to come? If it wasn't for Christian—you should have *told* me. How could I not come?"

"I don't know why I didn't tell you."

When we got home and got ready for bed, I offered him the option of sleeping with me or on the couch. I wasn't sure why I did that. To my surprise, he crawled into bed with me, and I turned out the light, unable to not think of the night I'd spent with Sam. I lay there on my back, careful not to brush up against Devin, trying to fall asleep, when the phone rang.

Oh shit. It was Sam.

We'd started calling each other right at bedtime just to say good night to each other. I said nothing, nor did I pick up the phone next to my bed. Instead, I let it ring until the machine picked up in the other room, and I could hear a muffled version of Sam's voice, "sweetheart" being the only word I made out clearly.

"I'm sorry about that, Dev," I said softly.

He didn't answer right away. He was so still that I could barely sense his presence. "It's OK," he said. "You could've answered it, you know."

"Not tonight," I replied.

Soon after, he spoke again.

"Did you miss your father? After he died, I mean."

"I really don't remember," I said. "I suppose that means I did."

"What if I don't miss him? What would that say about me?"

"You'll miss him," I said.

I then felt his shoulders bouncing, followed by the sound of restrained sobs. I leaned in and whispered, "It's OK," and with that permission, he broke down while I spooned him. I held him and stroked his hair, not unlike he did for me once.

His tears soon receded, followed by calm, even breathing. He then turned and looked at me. He looked innocent, almost childlike. He paused for a beat, and then he kissed me.

At first, his kiss was soft and soothing and gentle. Then he kissed me hard. Kissed me long and hard and slid his hands under my T-shirt and cupped my breasts, then grabbed my T-shirt from the inside and pulled it over my head. He pulled me close to him as I wrapped my arms around him and pulled off his T-shirt and started breathing heavily and climbed on top of him. Leaning over to the nightstand, I stretched to reach the drawer and pulled out a box of condoms that I had bought prior to my trip to see Sam, just in case. He then grabbed me and gently pushed me over and pinned me instead, kissing me again and moving first to my neck, and then to my breasts.

"What do you want?" I whispered in his ear.

He stopped and looked at me again. "I wanna make love to you," he said softly. He sounded needy.

How long had I waited for this? How often had I fanta-sized about what it would *feel* like? How long had I waited and searched and desperately yearned for the "right time," the "right place," and the "right man"? It all suddenly seemed like lost years. I'd tried to plan the moment as an *event*, something needing a fanfare, or flowers and candles, at least. Mark the date on my calendar, and observe it as an anniversary thereafter, a milestone. I'd always waited to be rescued from my demons, my shame, my insecurity, and expected sex to be the lifeboat. Was he my rescuer? Was he Prince Charming, literally? Just who was I making love to at this moment?

He is both the artist and the work of art. He sees beauty, he creates beauty, and he is beauty.

He is the lie that makes me realize the truth.

And then I knew: I didn't need the fanfare, didn't need to be rescued, didn't need to circle the date in red. I didn't need to be wooed and serenaded and gazed at with starry eyes. I didn't need satin sheets or chocolate kisses. Never. Perhaps I never even needed Devin. For the first time, I let go—truly let go of the lost years. I let go of Andrew and the others I'd briefly dated. I let go of my father's judgment, my mother's jealousy and indiffer-ence, and my brothers' armor. I let go of the woman who expended all her energy faking it, passing herself off as Andi, the savvy, sexy New Yorker who was great in bed and had men throwing themselves at her feet and never kissed and told. I had sex that night as if I'd been having it all along. As if I'd known how to all along. And perhaps I did.

Devin climaxed, and then rested his head on my shoul-der. We said nothing. Soon after, we did it again. We made love all night. As we began to drift into sleep, our warm bodies intertwined, I heard him faintly whisper, "Andrea."

"Dev," I whispered back in a sigh.

He kissed my cheek, cuddled close to me, and we slept soundly.

TWENTY-FIVE

Devin/David's Journal

I HAD BEEN WATCHING HER all day. Once, during the service, I turned my head and found her sitting several rows back, positioned in her seat so that she could see between two heads. She looked at the priest as if she were soaking in his voice like sunlight, but she must have felt my eyes watching her, for she suddenly met them and smiled warmly, and in that moment the rows disappeared and she was right beside me. Her hair was long and wavy, resting on her shoulders in wide ringlets that framed her elongated face. Her eyes flickered like a candle in the dimness of the cold church, amidst the sea of black. She kept her denim jacket over her shoulders and wore her violet V-neck sweater. I always liked the way that sweater looked on her, the way it accented her breasts, elongated her torso, and made her eyes look more blue than green, almost indigo.

I watched her again at my mother's house as she helped carry in and cover Pyrex dishes full of casseroles and pasta from the dining room to the kitchen, and throw out paper plates littered with scraps of food, unfinished salads, and half-bitten pieces of bread. Aunt Maria insisted that she didn't need to help with the cleanup, yet Andi continued helping anyway. I watched her smile shyly as she saran-wrapped dishes, and wondered if it was the light coming from the kitchen window that illuminated her skin and shined her honey-roasted chestnut hair. I studied her body—short, curved, and luxurious—as she stretched to reach the high shelves of cabinets, and surrendered to her stunted growth by leaving things on the counters when she couldn't, even in low heels and on tiptoes. Sacred in flesh, ample in bosom, masked in modern-day apparel: preserved.

I wondered: was she trying to get into my family's good graces? No. I had never formally invited her. Hadn't even called her—she showed up, much to my surprise, and informed me that she had to drag the information out of Christian, the rat-bastard. Perhaps she was like this at every family's post-funeral gathering, a people-pleaser who does what she thinks women should politely do. No. She'd told me stories about Thanksgiving dinner when she'd retire to the den with the rest of the guys to watch the Cowboys game, quickly dispelling (and resenting) the assumed gender roles and the notion that she was merely interested in Troy Aikman's butt. Besides, I knew her better than that.

But what captured me the most was when she crouched down on her knees, her long skirt covering her now-stocking feet, and knelt beside Meredith, who was spread out over a pad of paper and a box of half-spilled Crayolas as if they were classified blueprints. I couldn't hear what they were saying, but I watched Meredith trustingly allow Andi into her aura, pointing to her pictures, while Andi gave her complete attention. And I realized that Meredith was 3-dimensional and full of depth, fully visible and able to communicate, full of feeling and not removed from this world, this day, or this man who had touched her life as firmly and viscerally as he had touched every other person in the living room, the kitchen, the basement, the front porch, the house. And there was Andi, at Meredith's level, seeing the world, the day, and the man through those 5-year-old eyes; she had plenty to say, all the more wiser than Joannie, who was already pestering Mom to consider putting the house up for sale while the market was still hot. They had all abandoned this little girl in their efforts to shelter her from the silence. No wonder Meredith forgot that Andi started out a stranger. She must have seen the same assurance in Andi's eyes that I now saw: eyes that flicker in darkness, that find lost objects, that make diamonds look lackluster.

I watched all this and had to keep bringing myself back to my dead father, who by now lay—impatiently, I imagined—waiting to be lowered into the ground, next to my grandparents and great uncle. And I thought of the cold night air and shivered on the inside. I had to bring myself back to the bed of the next woman who lay—impatiently, I imagined—waiting for me to go down on her, safely, preplanned, and prepaid, and I kept hearing my father's words pound in me like a tribal rhythm: *"You're a good son. You're a man I'm proud to stand next to, because you're a man who has courage, who has respect, and brains, and who can tell his father to go to hell when his father is wrong."*

"I never told you to go to hell, Dad." Look at this, I'm still arguing with him, even now, I thought. *"And I never said you were wrong, either."*

"I was wrong to think you could be like me, and thank God you're no fag, or worse—a goddamn bloodsucking lawyer. But Jesus, David. You've got talent. You have more to give. You—now don't go crying on me now, boy. I'm only saying this 'cause it all suddenly makes sense. Son-of-a-bitch, what a rotten thing to do: give you all the answers right before you croak. Goddammit."

He said all this between broken breaths and morphine-induced stupors. I had to laugh to cover my tears.

"You'd better quit swearing, Dad, or else they might not let ya in."

"The hell with 'em."

My father grimaced in pain that he could no longer hide. In the midst of the silent scream, I sputtered out the words as he squeezed my hand in an effort to relieve some of his pain and avoid crying in weakness.

"I love you, Dad." I said it. Thank God I said it.

He gasped for air. *"I love you, too, David. Always have."*

She arrived knowing no one and left kissing everyone good-bye, wishing them well. Uncle Larry leaned over to me and practically whispered, "I don't know where you found her, but she's a real gem." And I had to shake my head and laugh to myself as I recalled that day and pictured myself trying to explain it. A gem, indeed. Now, in the car, I watched her drive, completely lost in the details of the day with fragments of words, waves of hair, and flickering eyes moving in the silence of the car and the blackness of the windows. We talked just a little bit, and she looked at me warmly, the same way as she did in the church, and with Meredith. Those blue-green marbles and thick lashes folded around me and pulled me inside their warmth. I wondered if this is what it feels like for women, if this is how they want to be enveloped by men after sex, to be pulled inside and then fully embraced and enveloped with all their love and security; to feel the touch, the actual, physical touch. What does that *feel* like? Is that what they really mean when they say, "Go inside me"? I needed to know.

That night, I crawled into bed with her beside me, breathed in the scent of her skin, and for a moment felt lightheaded with awe. She smelled so good, like lavender and vanilla. I'd spent nights with her before, lying next to her on the couch, feeling her feet brush against my leg, and knowing she was resisting the urge to snuggle close to me. Now I found myself trying to resist my own urges, and trembled at the very idea. What was happening to me? Should I sleep on the couch and risk hurting her feelings? She'd understand. After all, my father just died. I wasn't supposed to act as if everything were normal, as if everything were the same. We were never a couple. I had to constantly remind her of this when I caught her gazing into my eyes, or when she let her fingers slip through my hair almost automatically, or tried to kiss me. Don't fall for me, Andi. I said it the very first day. But I knew she fell for me the moment I puckered my lips and blew on her neck behind her ear, when we finally kissed, and when I went inside her safely, preplanned. I simply wouldn't allow myself to see it. For me, it had all been part of a day's work. Never mind that we took long walks in the park and spent hours in FAO Schwartz. Never mind that she dug listening to Thelonious Monk, or that she was giving me back something other than money. Something much more…

We spoke little, and when she turned out the light, I felt very alone and afraid. And it was then, in the darkness, without warning, that I began to sob uncontrollably, and seconds later I felt Andi's soft touch, like a silk scarf, on my shoulder and then across my back and she leaned in close and whispered, "It's OK." And in that instant I wasn't just crying for the loss of my father, but my lost boyhood, the missing affection and disconnection that echoed in hollowness all these years.

He did love me after all.

She continued to lean in and over me, across my back and around my shoulders, hovering and protecting me like trees do to children in a storm, stroking my hair. How I love when she strokes my hair.

Calmness started to overcome me like a passing cloud, and I began to feel very warm and full. We made love that night and it felt like it was my first time. It wasn't long before we drifted off to peaceful sleep under the soft bedding. She held me all night; it was my first full night's sleep in months.

TWENTY-SIX

As DEVIN SLEPT next to me, I carefully slid out of bed so as not to disturb him, picked up last night's T-shirt, which had been flung to the floor, and went to the bathroom. Afterwards, I crept into the kitchen and scavenged for food, finding little other than a box of stale Cocoa Puffs and leftover Chinese food, two eggs, and bread ends.

Great.

I don't think I realized until then just how much time I spent in the city. My apartment had been relegated to a rest stop, a place to sleep or change clothes. I had always rationalized that living on Long Island was cheaper than living in Manhattan or Brooklyn, but given my transit and dining expenses, I doubted that I at least broke even. No, I knew the real reason I chose Long Island when I moved back was because the city had scared me. Despite being a native New Yorker, I never really belonged there. Or so I thought.

What to do? Should I run out and buy bagels, leaving him a note? Should I wait for him to get up so we could go to breakfast together? Should I wake him up? Let him sleep?

I caught myself wishing that this sexual encounter had happened at his place rather than mine—it would've been easier for me to get away. *Easier for me to get away!* What was I thinking? I wondered, when it came to Devin, why was I always trying to escape? Or was that something I did with all men?

The more pressing question gnawing at me was whether I'd just cheated on Sam. I knew that when I'd said yes to the Northampton University gig, I'd also decided to commit to a serious relationship with Sam. Being that I hadn't actually made the move yet, and that Sam and I hadn't actually had sex yet, could I argue that the "serious" part of the relationship hadn't started yet? We weren't official (put another way, there was no contract). Had sleeping with Devin changed my wanting us to be? I knew that even if Sam hadn't come into my life, I still would've taken the new position. I was ready to move on. I needed to. That's what I had tried to explain to Devin at Junior's.

I looked at the answering machine light, blinking, Sam waiting to speak to me. I didn't play the message. I could tell him that I'd spent the night at Maggie's, I thought. Or should I tell him about Devin? I hadn't said anything so far, beyond the occasional vague allusion to this guy friend of mine. Sam once asked me if the guy friend was gay. When I told him no, he then asked if there was anything for him to worry about.

"Not anymore," I replied.

He pressed me, but I refused to elaborate, and eventually the subject faded.

No, we weren't official, I decided. And it would be a don't-ask-don't-tell policy.

Who was I kidding?

I changed my mind. The days of faking it were over, I decided.

Maybe Maggie and Jayce were right; maybe I was in love with both men.

As I sat on my loveseat and pondered all this, Devin wandered in, yawning and scratching his head, wearing the previous day's slacks and shirt opened and unbuttoned. He looked like he'd gone twenty rounds and lost.

"Morning," he said, startling me out of my thoughts.

"Hey, Dev."

We each remained frozen in our places, at a loss for words or the protocol for an escort and his friend with whom he'd just had sex for the first time. Finally, I stood up.

"How are you?" I asked, no sooner wishing I could pull the words back into my mouth.

"OK."

"How'd you sleep?"

"Fucking great."

"Good." I could tell he wanted to kiss me. Quite frankly, so did I. But neither of us moved.

"So, I don't really have much here in the form of breakfast," I said. "I could either make you some scrambled eggs or nuke some vegetable lo mein. Or we could go out to the diner, if you want."

"I should probably go back home—to my parents' house, I mean."

"Are you sure?"

"Yeah. I don't want my mom to be all alone so soon after."

"OK. I'll go change and drive you there."

"No need. I'll just get a cab."

"A cab'll clean you out."

"I'm good for it," he said, irked.

I fought the urge to be offended by his sarcasm, but failed. "Honestly, Dev, you're better off lighting a fucking match to your wallet. Case closed: I'm driving."

"Fine," he said, his voice mixed with defeat and defiance. "I'll get ready."

As he turned and headed back to my bedroom, a voice in my head shouted at me, *Don't let him walk away. Don't let him think you don't care, that it meant nothing to you...*

"Devin, wait," I called out, practically knocking him over as he stopped and pivoted while I threw my arms around him. He caught and embraced me tight, just as he had done at the funeral.

I let go and looked into his eyes, dim and depressed.

"Last night—" I started. He attempted to stifle me by putting his fingers to my lips, but I removed them and continued. "Last night was incredible. I'm so glad it was you. I mean that."

He tried to muster even just a little grin. "It was *you*, Andi." He embraced me again. "You gave me so much more."

"I just, I just wish it didn't happen this way, that's all," I said, my face muffled in his chest. "Under these circumstances."

"It is what it is," he said.

I fixed my eyes upon him, and we then simultaneously drew to each other like magnets and kissed.

We wanted each other all over again, I knew; yet we both let go as if by an involuntary reflex, a force of habit.

We were so used to pushing each other away that neither of us knew any other response. Or maybe we both knew last night was a one-time thing, and that I had already made up my mind. At the least, *I* knew.

We barely spoke in the car, just like the drive back from the funeral. When I pulled into the driveway of his parents' house, he drew in a breath, as if he were about to step into the ring and face the lions. Before he opened the door and stepped out, we faced each other one last time, our eyes focused in an earnest stare. I think it was the first time neither of us had anything to hide. And each saw a painful truth, indeed.

Devin gently caressed my cheek, and I returned the gesture, a tear escaping and sliding down and touching his finger. He smudged it away.

Without even saying good-bye, he got out of the car and didn't look back. And then, as I drove away, wiping yet another tear from my face, it hit me: in all the time we'd known each other, Devin and I never once had breakfast together.

TWENTY-SEVEN

June

D EVIN AND CHRISTIAN helped me load my furniture into the U-haul while Maggie and Jayce
labeled cartons. My car was filled to the brim; Sam had
agreed to wait for me at the Northampton apartment
he'd helped me find last month and help me unpack.
It'd been two weeks since Devin's father's funeral. He was
quiet all day, save take-charge, "get-it-done" commands
every now and then while the rest of us joked around and
Christian flirted with both Maggie and Jayce, trying to
recruit them as clients.

I had said good-bye to my mother the day before after
having dinner at her house. My brothers Joey and Tony
were playing gigs on the road. One in Philadelphia and
the other in Chicago. My good-byes to Jayce and Maggie
(especially Maggie) were long and tearful. I also thanked
Christian and gave him a hug.

"Stay cool," he said. I returned his words with a wink.

Devin and I stood outside, alone, and faced each other.
We had said little to each other all day, and hadn't seen
each other since the night we spent together after the
funeral. A light breeze blew as the late afternoon sun
peeked in and out of passing clouds.

"Thank you for everything," I said quietly.

He looked down and stared at the asphalt driveway without answering me.

"You know," I said, "we never got a chance to talk about any of this."

"What's there to talk about? You made your choice."

Where had I heard that before?

"I don't know how you feel about it."

He laughed one of those laughs of exasperation as he shook his head and rolled his eyes.

"You don't know how I fucking feel about it…geez, Andi."

"What."

"I'm in love with you."

My jaw dropped.

"What?"

"You heard me."

I fumed to the point where I thought I actually felt smoke come out of my ears.

"*Now* you tell me this?"

"I've been a little distracted lately."

"Ya couldn't slip it in somewhere?"

"When—as my father was going into the ground? Between gag reflexes over my aunt's fucking stale casserole?"

"How 'bout the day I told you at Junior's? How 'bout the night we…"

"I didn't know then."

"You didn't know then? When did you have this epiphany?"

"I don't know."

I paused.

"I can't help but notice that you're back to work, so maybe you're not all that distracted after all."

"Don't you dare make this about my work."

I paused again, the awkward silence wafting through the breeze like an overturned garbage pail.

"So, how am I to respond to this confession?" I asked.

"How should I know?"

"What do you want me to say?"

"Forget it, Andi. Just get in your car and go."

I looked away for a second, drew in a breath, and looked back at him.

"You know, for someone who has all the right words to sweep a woman off her feet, you really suck at this."

"Nice fucking good-bye."

"No, I mean it," I said, raising my voice. "What are you so afraid of, Dev? You know, you've never really been honest with me. You've extolled the virtues of my body and my sexuality, and you complimented me on my kissing and you've written some excellent pieces. But you've never told me what you *think*. What you *feel*. Did you think I wouldn't approve of you either?"

"Would it have made you stay?"

"Maybe!"

"Oh *bullshit*, Andi!" The volume of his voice matched mine. "You said yourself that you don't approve of what I do for a living. Hell, you just insinuated it two minutes ago with that smarmy, righteous tone of yours!"

"I never said I don't approve—I said I could never accept it if we were together!"

"Whatever. Gimme a break with splitting the fucking semantic hairs. And don't you preach to me about honesty! You're the one who kept this little secret from me and dropped it on my balls like a dumbbell! In fact, *you* keep secrets very well."

"I was sorry about that, Devin." My voice softened. "You know that."

"David."

The word stopped us both in our tracks.

"What did you say?"

"My name is *David.*"

"I don't know David."

We looked into each other's eyes for a moment, and then I shifted back to the pavement—the hurt I saw was too much for me to bear. I kicked pebbles on the ground.

"I don't want to say good-bye this way," I said softly as a tear rolled down my cheek and dropped onto the pavement, marking a dot. "I don't want it to end like this."

"I don't want it to end at all," he said.

We looked at each other again. He took my hand. "Please don't go," he pleaded, his voice breaking on the first word.

"I have to go, and this has to end," I said, looking at my hand in his.

"Why?"

"Because it was a lie."

He paused to ponder this.

"Not all of it."

"Too much of it."

"So, we can start over."

"As what? Friends? Lovers? What are we now—the escort and his former client? I can't and I don't want to start over. I want to start something new with someone else."

"God, don't do this to me, Andi. Please. Not right now."

I caressed his face with my free hand. "I don't want to hurt you."

He took hold of me and kissed me hard. My body surged—dammit, I felt that kiss in my toenails. We embraced in a way we'd never done before, kissing and clinging to each other. My mind raced while my body throbbed: *Maybe I don't have to leave. Maybe I could unpack the U-haul tomorrow, call NU, and tell them I changed my mind. Then I could call Mags and tell her not to give Sarah the keys to my office just yet. I could e-mail Sam and tell him…what could I tell him? That I just met…that I was going back to…that I was starting…*

I kissed him one last time.

"I'll always love you, Dev, and I'll always be grateful to you."

"David," he corrected me again, even more painfully than the first time, still holding my hand.

I repeated, more painfully than the first time, "I don't know David."

"I want you to," he said in almost a whisper.

I stood on my toes and spoke in his ear. "Then start *being* David."

He held onto my hand. I used my other to unclasp his, and then backed up to my car.

"Will you get back to the city OK?" I asked. He nodded, his eyes glassy. I got into the car and waved.

"Good-bye."

He raised and lowered his hand in a rapid gesture. "Bye," he barely uttered.

I spent the drive listening to a book on tape and breaking out in tears for several stretches at a time. Thanks to a car accident on the Throgs Neck Bridge, rush hour traffic on I-95 through Hartford, and construction just past Providence, I didn't arrive at my new apartment until midnight. Sam was there, wide awake, with a carpet picnic awaiting me. Both his presence and thoughtfulness reassured me almost immediately.

"Welcome home, sweetheart," he said warmly.

Physically and emotionally exhausted, all I could manage was a sigh.

TWENTY-EIGHT

October — Sixteen Months Later

S EX WITH SAM is fucking fabulous.
I'm not sure I have any point of reference beyond
Devin; I'm not even sure it's a matter of comparison.
Nevertheless, this has been the case since day one. Or
night four, depending on how you look at it.

Night one, the night I'd arrived in Northampton, I
crashed on the air mattress Sam had prepared for me. He
crashed with me. Night two, I crashed again, this time on
my own mattress, after spending the entire day unpacking
boxes and moving furniture, with Sam's help, of course.
He crashed with me again.

Night three, I had a temporary meltdown, one of those
moments when you realize the enormity and possible stupidity of what you've just done—moved to a new city and
state (even if it was a state in which you used to live); left
behind your comfortable, familiar job and friends and
family (again); and left behind a guy you-were-friends-with-
and-sort-of-seeing-but-not-really-but-ended-up-sleeping-
with-but-it-didn't-work-out-but-maybe-you-should've-tried.
I suddenly looked at Sam as if he were a stranger and
decided I'd made a mistake, my mind's eye seeing Devin
standing in the driveway of my East Meadow apartment,

defeated. "Go away," I said to Sam, or something to that effect. He understood, wonderful creature that he is, and left me to sleep in what was suddenly a big, empty bed, and it was only a full-size mattress. He wasn't mad or anything. Just smiled and hugged me and left.

By night four, I'd regained my senses. It happened while I was alone in my apartment, setting up my office space. All it took was the thought of Sam's hug: he holds either firmly in an assuring way or squeezes cuddly-like. When I'd sent him away the night before, he did both. This time, I called him: "Get over here." He came over and I yanked him through the doorway before he even had a chance to knock and pulled him into the bedroom and took leave of all inhibition. Just like that. (I couldn't help but think that Devin the Escort would've been proud.) Granted, Sam and I had been talking about it ever since that night in front of the fireplace during spring break weekend, when he said he wanted us to wait. We'd exchanged e-mails and phone calls inquiring what kind of sex we wanted and how we wanted our first time to be and what we each liked and didn't like, and I even put Devin's claim of "you can't have good sex if you can't talk about good sex" to use by challenging Sam to respond to it, to which he rose to the challenge by producing a four-page essay, citing sources and everything.

On night four, we did everything we'd talked about, and some things we didn't, and haven't been able to keep our damn hands off each other since. And what amazed me was how *easy* it was for me—natural, I mean. As if I'd never had a single insecurity about sex. As if I'd been having sex throughout my adult life. As if Sam and I had known each other throughout the duration of our lives. I wondered who was to get the credit for this: Was it Sam, with his way of making me feel so at home? What did he have that Andrew and the others didn't? Or was it Devin, for teaching me how to make me feel at home myself? Or had I simply been there all along?

Regardless of the answer, sex with Sam is fucking fabulous.

I suppose sex with Sam is so fabulous because Sam is fabulous. He cooks, for one thing. Makes French toast for dinner, smoothies for breakfast, and vegetable soup from scratch for lunch, among other things. I've taken to baking lately—even tried cheesecake in response to his chicken parmesan. He loves my cupcakes.

Sam also reads to me. I'd forgotten how much I love to be read to, something my brothers used to do for me when we were kids, before they had gigs or rehearsals or lessons to run off to. Sam reads everything to me, from novels to newspaper articles to selected student papers. He has a beatific reading voice and, like my brothers used to, often makes up voices for characters or narrators. Sometimes I get so swept away by his rounded tones and placid articulations that I forget to listen to the content. In the early days, Sam's reading made me horny as hell—one time, while reading a section of Bill Bryson's *A Walk in the Woods* in which Bryson expounds on the history of the park rangers, Sam put the book down and looked at me.

"Sweetheart, are you listening to me?" he asked.

I pounced on him like a cat does a toy mouse laced with catnip.

By the end of my first semester at NU, I had moved out of my apartment and into Sam's house, delighted by how quickly "his" became "ours": hardwood floors, earthy-colored walls, and lots of bookcases. We literally picked out curtains together, along with plush, coffee house–style sofas and bistro chairs and tables. And we got a cat—a mixed breed of orange tabby and tuxedo that we named "Donny Most" (after the guy who played Ralph Malph on the old *Happy Days* series). We even shared the same sense of humor.

And Sam makes me laugh constantly.

Not to say that we don't have a couple of knockdown, drag-out fights once in a while. Not to say that my demons (or his) don't show up uninvited now and then. Not to say Sam isn't stubborn as hell, a hopeless pack rat, and stingy with the butter when he cooks. Worse yet, he's high maintenance while trying to pass himself off as low maintenance—it became clear early on that we were going to need our own bathrooms. But we write apology letters in the form of memoirs or allegories and leave them on the bedside tables. We sit and talk until our throats are dry and/or we reach consensus. Sam is patient and understanding. He listens. And I listen to him in ways I never listened to my exes. Perhaps because I know him better than I ever knew them. Or perhaps because I've gotten so good at silencing the voices of self-judgment that kept me from truly hearing anyone else.

Besides, I'd discovered the joys of make-up sex, so even fighting with Sam proved fabulous in the end.

I not only fell in love with Sam, but I fell in love with New England all over again, and saw it with new eyes:

Manhattan without her makeup on. Low maintenance Long Island. Trails and trees offset by hills and mountains flanked by sand and sea. We frequently took little trips to Boston and Cape Cod and New Hampshire and Vermont.

By the end of my second semester at NU, Sam asked me to marry him, and I accepted.

Yet, despite all this bliss, I occasionally found myself missing Devin.

So many times I thought about calling him, or writing a letter and actually mailing it, apologizing for the way things ended between us that day in East Meadow. I would often think about the things we used to do together. It all seemed like another lifetime, and when I imagined him with his clients, I no longer felt the sickening jealousy in the pit of my stomach. In fact, I had adopted the classic Devin mentality: business as usual. He had sex with these women. He might not have technically consummated these relationships with copulation, but he had sex with every last one of them. He seduced them or submitted to their seductions, danced around them with foreplay, and indulged them in their hedonistic fantasies. It's all perfectly acceptable to me now. And indeed, I was one of them, and OK with that, too. And I imagined myself going back, every now and then, to Café Dante on Bleaker Street and asking Dev for pointers on fantasy play.

I missed his charm and wit. I missed his chiseled features. I missed his coy wink. I missed our conversations and banter. I missed seeing him in his boxers. I missed the comfort level we'd reached with each other.

But being with Sam also made me realize how Devin and I had barely scratched the surface of a relationship. For all we had exposed, we also withheld. For all we gave, we also kept to ourselves. We'd passed up so many opportunities to be intimate that when we finally slept together, we were strangers.

I didn't tell Sam about sleeping with Devin. I wasn't deliberately keeping it a secret—I simply didn't know what to say. Devin and I were more like fictional characters than actual people. We were artifacts, creations of each other's imaginations. Friends and lovers and teachers and escorts.

Sam and I had a three-day weekend for Columbus Day and decided to spend it in Boston. We arrived Friday afternoon and stayed at a friend's apartment in the North End. That night we dined at an Italian restaurant down the street that took me back twenty years to my grandmother's Queens kitchen. I introduced Sam to gnocchi; in gratitude, he bought me flowers that turned the head of every Bostonian who passed us on the street.

Late Saturday morning, after breakfast, Sam perused the *Boston Leisure Weekly*, a local community paper, while I did dishes.

"Hey, sweetheart, listen to this," he said, and read aloud:

Life can be a series of happy mistakes.

I was still new to the Boston area (and its art scene) when I decided to check out the Senior Art Show at the Boston School of Art.

Keep in mind that I'm a relocated New Yorker. Manhattan, to be exact. I'd gotten used to grids. I'd gotten used to numerical progressions, to cross-street references (Fifty-seventh and Fifth, Seventh and Lex). I'd gotten used to dichotomies: East and West, Upper and Lower, Uptown and Downtown. So you can imagine what a city like Boston does to a guy's sense of direction. How many times have I gone in circles only to find that my intended destination was right down the block?

And so, after a series of wrong turns and getting caught in a downpour, I conceded that I was lost yet again and stumbled into what turned out to be a belly dancing class to ask for directions. The cymbal-clicking, veil-waving temptresses were actually a group of printmaking students who privately met once a week to "unleash their inner goddesses." And although the dancing was certainly an art form unto itself and undoubtedly worthy of my attention, it was not what I had in mind. So I politely (and soggily) declined their offer to join their group, and instead thanked them, heading out once again.

Quickly dismissing an image of my soaking body flopping and gyrating, surrounded by printmaking belly dancers, I'd hoped I was getting close, until I passed a propped door with a brushed bronzed plaque that read *Graduate Gallery*. This was still not my final destination, but the low lighting and satisfying purr of the air-conditioner drew me in, and once inside, I almost immediately felt a shift in reality. A sign near the gallery's entrance introduced me to the collection by Jesse Bartlett, and I decided to stay and get acquainted. Together, the paintings displayed a balance of the energy, movement, and warm, earthy colors of the cave paintings of Lascaux partnered with the edge of modern city life and a skilled, albeit young, hand.

Each piece contains its own voice, its own message. A fragment of city life as seen, experienced, and recorded from every angle and position imaginable. Twenty-six-year-old Bartlett brings a unique perspective to his paintings. "City life was unlike anything I'd ever seen before," says the Granby, Vermont, native who relocated to Boston for his graduate work in contemporary painting. "It was just raw, and I was blown away by it. Blindsided, you know? And everybody just walks around like nothing's happening. And I just stop and stare," he shrugs, "because it's all I can do."

"And then you paint," I respond.

"Yeah. I paint what I see, and what other people don't see. 'Cause you got to see this, and you got to see it for what it is."

"So, what is 'it'?"

"Life," he says simply. "People. The good stuff."

Like their subjects, these paintings are innately beautiful—abstract, literal, human, and personal. They are also rough and textured, unbalanced, and sometimes even harsh. Viewing this art feels almost voyeuristic, much like seeing everything about a person in one glance. Process and narration are evident in each piece. Layers of weathered newspapers, flyers, and found objects are washed with color to construct the scaffolding behind a strong drawing hand and confident use of color, shape, and form. The subject and material blend in formal voice, creating a texture and even scent of life. Individually, these pieces are sensual; together, they are compelling.

The images aren't clean, they aren't perfect, and they aren't always refined. But they are real. They are telling. Alive. The show comes together in a world of tone, light, and atmosphere. It gets under your skin until it seeps out of your hair. You *feel* this art. To view it is to truly experience city life, be it Boston or the Big Apple. And it feels good. Pleasurable.

Jesse Bartlett has something to say, and he is just beginning to learn how to say it. He's the kind of artist you'll want to discuss someday at a cocktail party, bragging that you knew him when. And you'll have every right to brag, because he's worth the experience. You won't forget it. Neither will I.

And neither, hopefully, will those belly dancers.

Unlike previous bouts of reading bliss, this time I hung off every word. I'd heard this style before, I was sure of it—the words, the rhythm, the voice. But where? Was it at a conference? In a journal article? A student paper?

"Cool, huh?" said Sam. "A bit of overkill, maybe, but vivid. Let's go see this exhibit, OK? It's at a gallery on Beacon Street."

"Who wrote it?" I asked. Before he could answer, the phone rang. Sam jumped up to answer it, still holding the paper in his hand, now closed and rolled into a cylinder. He handed off the phone to me, and I forgot about the review and its unknown author.

———

We took the T to the Park Street stop and walked the rest of the way. Early evening had settled in, and a chilly autumnal breeze whistled its arrival. Sam and I huddled close and walked quickly, almost passing the entrance to the Paris Gallery, its name embossed on the squeaky glass door in simple, gold block letters. The gallery was a small loft space on the second floor with buffed, honey-colored hardwood floors and well-lit, white walls showcasing a collection of prints and paintings. The exhibit had officially opened the night before, but a reception was already underway for tonight as well. I spied a man wearing a black blazer, ripped jeans, and a T-shirt with a silkscreen print—I correctly guessed him to be Jesse Bartlett. He stood near one of his more elegant, yet darker paintings, a flute of champagne in one hand, an unlit cigarette in the other, his eyes hidden behind long, bleached bangs, talking to a rather blond couple.

Sam and I circled the gallery, spending time in front of each frame. We'd been to exhibits together before, but none matched the experience I'd had at any museum or gallery with Devin. Viewing a work of art with Devin was practically a spiritual experience; I could transcend time and space with him, and every time he would show me a new way of seeing, ways I think even Picasso never would have thought of. And it wasn't just Devin's knowledge that made those visits so enlightening; witnessing his own transcendence from *seeing* to *being* was equally illuminating.

A hushed chatter filled the gallery, and I felt a sense of belonging. "I like it here," I heard myself say to Sam in a quiet, calm voice. He didn't respond. A pretty woman in her early twenties approached us with a tray of champagne flutes and offered one to each of us. Sam took one while I graciously refused, asking for a ginger ale instead. She offered to check for me.

Just as we finished viewing the final painting, I sensed someone behind me and turned around: my vision fixated on the flute of ginger ale first, followed by the cuff of a Versace jacket sleeve, up the sleeve to the shoulder, and finally to the face, meeting sparks of sienna.

"This has to be for you," he said, holding out the glass.

TWENTY-NINE

I BECAME A SCULPTURE.

Devin.

He extended his hand to Sam. "Hi, I'm David Santino, co-owner of the gallery."

David.

"Sam Vanzant," he said as he shook hard, "and this is my fiancée, Andrea Cutrone." Devin—David—took my hand into his own, gently.

"It's nice to see you, Andi."

For the moment he seemed unfazed by Sam's introduction of me as his fiancée. But Sam perked upon hearing him refer to me as "Andi" and looked first at me, then at him, then back at me.

"You two know each other?"

I tried to speak, honestly. Opened my mouth, but an incomprehensible dribble not unlike a failing ignition starter emanated instead of words.

"I...eyuttuttuttya...eeya..."

"We had mutual friends at Brooklyn U," Devin—David—said.

Past tense?

"Really?" Sam replied, continuing the conversation. "Sweetheart, you didn't tell me you know the owner here."

"Oh, I've only been here for about six or seven months. Georgia Paris is the other owner." He pointed to a classy, silver-haired woman who had joined Jesse Bartlett and the blond couple. "I sold my other business, sublet my apartment in the city, moved here, and became a partner. Georgia's teaching me everything she knows so I can take over."

He was responding to Sam but looking at me. I could feel my pupils dilating, my sockets widening as he spoke the words "my *other* business."

"What'd you do before?" Sam asked.

Wait for it…

"I was in the service industry." He winked at me. Rat-bastard—he deliberately left himself wide open. I swore the hardwood floor was quicksand and I'd just sunk down to my knees.

"Well, fancy meeting us here. Small world," Sam replied.

"He knew the dean." I finally stammered an answer to a question long gone. Both men looked at me, perplexed. "At Brooklyn U." I turned to Devin. "Didn't you?"

He grinned. "You look great."

"So do you," I replied, my face flushed, my insides stirring. "I almost didn't recognize you." I was meeting him for the first time all over again and reacting the exact same way: clumsy and bumbling and exhilarated all at once. "David," I said out loud, a reminder to myself. This was whom I was meeting.

"So, whaddya think of the exhibit?"

"Good stuff," Sam said, taking a quick look around. "We read a great review of it in the *Boston Leisure Weekly* this morning, and it was dead-on accurate."

"Thanks—I wrote it."

How could I not have known? How could I not have even guessed?

"Oh my God—it was YOU!!!"

My exclamation turned heads. I regained solid ground again, alert and at attention.

"Yes, Andi. I'm a writer now, too. I have an occasional review in the *Boston Leisure*. I'm trying to make it into a regular column, though. Still an amateur, I guess."

"You were always a writer," I insisted, echoing a familiar voice from a previous time in a previous relationship.

"Well, you've got a flair for narrative," said Sam. "Andi and I are both memoirists."

"Yes, and I happen to know that *she* is quite talented," said Devin, still grinning. Didn't his cheekbones hurt?

I beamed while my heart pounded, and Sam put his arm around me and pulled me towards him, giving me a proud kiss that was intended for my cheek but instead reached my right temple. "You got that right," he said.

After a quick pause in the conversation, Sam asked Devin the way to the men's room, then excused himself.

"So…" I started. He knew what was coming. "You really left the business, huh."

"Yep."

"How come?"

"You know, it's funny. I swore the only reason I'd ever stop being an escort was because I'd lost a limb—certainly not because of some moral conscience."

"You had a moral conscience?"

He flirtatiously cocked an eyebrow, which broke my straight face.

"Actually, I stopped enjoying it. Doing it just got more and more pointless—not for them, but for me. There didn't seem to be anything for me to want anymore."

"When'd you stop?"

"'Bout a year ago, I think. Shortly after you left."

"What'd you do?"

"I divested myself from the business, turned it over to Christian, and I had a shitload of cash laying around, so I decided to take a long vacation in Europe. Italy, Spain, France, you name it. I found every big museum and back-street gallery imaginable. Even got robbed one time, smack in the middle of the day, although I only had a couple of travelers' cards and the equivalent of fifty bucks on me... Ya know, American Express really is good about getting stolen cards replaced."

Sam returned before I could continue the conversation, and Devin reached into his pocket. "Here." He pulled out a business card and handed it to me. "I'm almost always here. Give me a call and we'll have lunch sometime."

I took the card and studied the number and had to look twice at the name: *David Santino*. I still wasn't used to it.

"Thanks." My voice sounded distant.

"Well, I've got to tend to my patrons. Thanks so much for coming." He shook Sam's hand again. "It was a pleasure to meet you."

"Same here."

He turned to me. "And so nice to see you again."

"Welcome to New England," I said and winked. A final smile erupted from him, and he crossed the floor to schmooze with another couple.

Sam turned to me. "How 'bout that," he said.

"Indeed."

I sipped my ginger ale.

"Sweetheart, what are you smiling at?"

THIRTY

W E SAT at a table in a Peruvian coffeehouse down the road from the Paris Gallery in Boston two weeks later. We laughed when we saw each other, both dressed in faded T-shirts, jeans, and leather jackets. He eyed the diamond and sapphire ring on my left finger.

"When'd you get engaged?"

"End of May."

"Hm." He nodded. "Seems like a good guy."

"He is."

David dug his fork into the slice of fudge cake we were sharing.

"I think it's great that you're writing," I said.

"I kept a journal the entire time I was in Europe. I wrote a lot about my father and growing up, and about you, too."

Tears watered my eyes.

"And then, one day all I wanted to do was paint. There I was in Positano, completely lost in the sunset, dying for a set of oils. And then, it came to me—and I swear it was in my father's voice: 'You're an artist, David.' And that was it. I came home."

"Then how come you're not painting now? I mean, you're a gallery owner instead."

"Because for me, the true love isn't in making the art; it's being surrounded by it. I once had a client who had a brother who worked in a bookstore. She said he could have easily been the next Vonnegut or Ellison, but he absolutely loved being around the books. That's what felt like home to him."

I understood.

"And that's what the gallery feels like to me. For me, art is born out of my witness. I guess it's the same with you and memoir."

"Precisely. I suppose that's why I've always loved rhetoric—it's always in response to something else."

"I can write about it, talk about it, see it. Might as well show it and sell it too, because I also do that very well."

"Ya sure do. So…I guess you left New York because of Devin?"

"A city of eight million people—you'd be surprised how often I would run into my fucking clients."

"Why Boston?"

"Good art scene. Good city. Good opportunities. I met Georgia, one thing led to another, and the rest is history."

I sat quietly, taking long and slow bites of cake.

"Do you ever miss being an escort?" I finally asked.

He bit his lip and shook his head. "Surprisingly not. Do you ever miss being in New York?"

"Surprisingly not."

We sat and stared and smiled at each other.

"Do you ever miss *me*, Andi?"

I studied the cake crumbs on my crumpled napkin and didn't answer.

"Why'd you call me?" he asked.

"I'm not sure."

"I'm glad you did."

"Do you ever miss *me*?" I asked.

He blushed and grinned again and took his final bite of cake.

"So when's the wedding?" he asked.

"Next October," I replied. "A year from now."

"Hm," he answered. "Not June, when school's out?"

"We both wanted an autumn wedding."

I paused.

"Are you seeing anyone?" I asked.

"Not right now. I mean, I've been dating, but nothing's stuck so far. I'd like to, though. Get into a serious relationship, I mean."

We paused again, and David looked at his watch.

"I gotta get back to the gallery."

We left the coffeehouse and walked down the street, stopping at the corner. The sun brightly blazed over Boston, framed by a cobalt blue sky. I felt toasty in my leather jacket and squinted through my shades. I looked up at him, remembering how tall and towering he could be.

"I'm glad you called," he said again. He took me into his arms and held me close.

"Oh, Dev," I practically cried into his jacket. "I do miss you."

His scent reawakened strong memories.

"I miss you too," he said, stroking my hair.

He kissed me gingerly on my forehead. I looked at him through glassy eyes and iridescent lenses.

"See ya, David."

"See ya."

I began to walk away.

"Hey, Andi!" he called as I turned the corner. I spun around and he quickly caught up to me and leaned in close. "I gotta ask: how's the sex with Sam?"

"Fucking fabulous."

Neither of us could conceal our delight.

"That's cute," he replied.

We each turned the corner and walked away, in opposite directions.

ACKNOWLEDGMENTS

This book could not have been born without the following people:

First and foremost, thank you to Stacey Cochran, who introduced me to and mentored me through the community of published writing and writers.

Thanks also to Neil Coleman, the very first person to read the manuscript in its first incarnation, and to subsequent readers, including (in alphabetical order) Evelyn Audi, Celeste Girrell, Mary Gonzalez, John Griffin, Linda Licata, Ariel Lorello, Katie Marciano, Crystal Medeiros, Tracy Branco Medeiros, Susan Miller-Cochran, Kelly Sutphin, Bruce W. Tench II, Marisa Von Beeden, and all of my students and others who were kind enough to listen to excerpts and tell me what they thought.

Thanks to Elisa DiLeo, who helped me find my way around Manhattan, and Richard Romero, owner of Mirasol's café in North Dartmouth, Massachusetts, where most of this book was written and discussed over countless cups of vanilla chai latte.

Thanks to Dr. John Caruso, who advised me in college that sport psychology was not the way to go, and to Drs. W. Keith Duffy and Mary Hallct, who took me under their wings in grad school and married me to rhetoric and composition.

Thank you always to my mother, Eda, my father, Michael, my grandmother, Mary Mottola, my brothers, sister, and extended family for their unending support, especially my twin brother, Paul, who is a much better writer than I am and constantly raises the bar.

To all those well-established writers who inspire me and make me laugh on a regular basis, especially Aaron Sorkin and Nora Ephron, and to writer/scholar Peter Elbow and the late Donald Murray, I bow to you.

Finally, a special thank you to Sarah Girrell Paquette, whom I adore. Without her insight, feedback, knowledge of art, and love for this book, Devin and Andi never would have stood a chance.

2010 Addendum:

Thank you to Terry Goodman and AmazonEncore for being so enthusiastic about *Faking It* and wanting to share it with the world. I couldn't ask for a more committed and class-act publisher.

ABOUT THE AUTHOR

Photo Credit: Larry H. Leitner, 2010

Elisa Lorello was born and raised on Long Island, the youngest of seven children. She earned her bachelor's and master's degrees from the University of Massachusetts-Dartmouth and eventually launched a career in rhetoric and composition studies. She has been teaching first-year writing to university students since 2000. Elisa currently resides in North Carolina, where she splits her time between teaching and writing. *Faking It* is her first novel.

To learn more about Elisa and her other writing projects, please visit her blog *"I'll Have What She's Having": The Official Blog of Elisa Lorello* at www.elisalorello.blogspot.com, or her official Web page at www.elisalorello.com.